A SMIDGEN OF
SHAKESPEARE

Also available

A Smattering of Latin

Geoff Spiteri

A SMIDGEN OF SHAKESPEARE

PORTICO

Published in the United Kingdom in 2016 by
Portico Books
1 Gower Street
London
WC1E 6HD

An imprint of Pavilion Books

ISBN 978-1-91023-299-6

A CIP catalogue record for this book is available from the British Library.

10 9 8 7 6 5 4 3 2 1

Reproduction by Mission Productions Ltd, Hong Kong
Printed and bound by 1010 Printing International Ltd, China

This book can be ordered direct from the publisher.
Contact the marketing department, but try your bookshop first.

www.pavilionbooks.com

CONTENTS

And seeing ignorance is the curse of God,
Knowledge the wing wherewith we fly to heaven

Lord Say, Henry VI Part II, Act IV, scene vii

DOES SHAKESPEARE MATTER?

In a survey commissioned for the National Year of Reading, teenagers were asked about their most and least favourite things to read. Top of the popular list were gossip magazines, with online computer game cheats and *Harry Potter* not far behind. Top of the most loathed reads was homework, with the runner-up spot taken by the collected works of one William Shakespeare.

However, it is not only teenagers who feel like this about the Great Bard. For many of us Shakespeare boils down to a few hazily remembered plots and one or two of the more famous lines that pretty much everyone can misquote. The mere mention of the author's name may revive memories of long, arduous – if not downright boring – lessons spent attempting to translate arcane, 400-year-old words and phrases into modern English. The experience will often have been frustrating – with only occasional flashes of the playwright's brilliance illuminating what felt like a long twilight of tedium.

For most of us things probably won't have changed much as we've got older. We may have forced ourselves to re-read the occasional play. Or perhaps we've fidgeted our way through a theatre production or film version of one of the plays.

The question, then, is whether Shakespeare is still worth the effort. Is it really worth the bother of reading plays and poetry written in obscure language that hardly anyone these days can understand straight off?

The answer is yes – and the reasons are numerous.

One reason, as your English teacher will no doubt have told you when you were studying Shakespeare in the classroom for the first time, is that 'the Bard' is now considered so important that he belongs to everybody. In common with only a few of the world's greatest artists and thinkers – Michelangelo, Beethoven, Voltaire, Picasso – Shakespeare now transcends national borders and belongs to the whole of humanity. Wikipedia describes Shakespeare as 'the greatest writer in the English language and the world's pre-eminent dramatist'. Google lists 68,200,000 entries for William Shakespeare, while his works have been translated into more than 70 of the world's languages, including Latin, ancient Greek and even Klingon. A truly enormous secondary publishing industry has built up around his name and his work (this book is an example). Familiarity with those 37 plays, 154 sonnets and other surviving works will place you very firmly in the company of the millions of other people on this earth who 'get' and appreciate Shakespeare.

Another reason is that, although Shakespeare's poetry and plays were written over 400 years ago, they still resonate with remarkable insight into what it means to be human. You want to gain some understanding of jealousy? Read *Othello*. You want advice on the art of seduction? *Richard III* has some great lines. You want anguish, fear, anger? Try *Hamlet*. The best of his characters are real and complex individuals who stay in our minds: Leontes is cruel, Lady Macbeth is ambitious, Iago is Machiavellian.

In the four centuries since Shakespeare was writing, the human condition has not changed. The same truths that held true then hold true today. In this sense the plays and poems can be seen as a vast repository of human experience that speaks clearly to us today.

A third reason that Shakespeare still matters is the wealth and sheer unadulterated joy and inventiveness of the language he used. You only need to be aware of how many Shakespearean phrases have been passed down into modern English to appreciate this. To take just a couple of examples, the phrase 'winter of discontent', much loved by tabloid headline writers, is a direct quote from the opening scene of *Richard III*:

> **Now is the winter of our discontent**
> **Made glorious summer by this sun of York;**
> **And all the clouds that lour'd upon our house**
> **In the deep bosom of the ocean buried.**

'Parting is such sweet sorrow', likewise, comes from Act II, scene ii of *Romeo and Juliet*:

> **Good night, good night! Parting is such**
> **sweet sorrow,**
> **That I shall say good night till it be**
> **morrow.**

Or how about this one: 'The course of true love never did run smooth'? It comes from Act I, scene i of *A Midsummer Night's Dream*:

> **Ay me! for aught that I could ever read,**
> **Could ever hear by tale or history,**
> **The course of true love never did run smooth.**

And all this really is just the tip of the iceberg. Anyone re-reading the plays and the sonnets will stumble across literally hundreds of words and phrases recognizable in our own modern-day lexicon. For this reason alone it is well worth revisiting his work.

Shakespeare remains a great national symbol whose words inspired Danny Boyle's spectacular Opening Ceremony for the London 2012 Olympic Games. The event was launched by cyclist Bradley Wiggins striking the huge Olympic Bell, forged in Whitechapel in east London and engraved with a quote from *The Tempest*: 'Be not afeard. The isle is full of noises.' The dramatic people's history that unfolded, blending humour, emotion and magic, celebrated enduring icons of Britishness – from Shakespeare, Blake and Milton to Isambard Kingdom Brunel, David Bowie and Sir Tim Berners-Lee. It was a feast for eyes and ears, with Caliban's speech, delivered by the actor Kenneth Branagh, providing a powerful underlying theme for the magnificent display:

> **Be not afeard. The isle is full of noises,**
> **Sounds, and sweet airs, that give delight,**
> **and hurt not.**
> **Sometimes a thousand twangling instruments**
> **Will hum about mine ears; and sometime voices,**
> **That, if I had then wak'd after long sleep,**
> **Will make me sleep again; and then, in dreaming,**
> **The clouds methought would open and show riches**
> **Ready to drop upon me, that, when I wak'd,**
> **I cried to dream again.**

At the start of the twenty-first century, 400 years after his death, Shakespeare's voice still captures the imagination and speaks to the world.

So the short answer is that someone such as Shakespeare, with so much 'brand recognition' and continued relevance, deserves at least some working knowledge on our part. The good news is that the days of sloughing through acres and acres of set texts are over. Clearly nothing will replace a good knowledge of the original works, but the following guide will provide something of a shortcut to understanding why, and how, Shakespeare still matters.

1
'THE PLAY'S THE THING'

OPENING LINES

Here's a selection of some of the better-known opening lines
from Shakespeare's plays:

O! for a Muse of fire, that would ascend
The brightest heaven of invention.
Henry V

When shall we three meet again?
In thunder, lightning, or in rain?
Macbeth

Now is the winter of our discontent
Made glorious summer by this sun of York.
Richard III

If music be the food of love, play on;
Give me excess of it, that, surfeiting,
The appetite may sicken, and so die.
Twelfth Night

THE SHORTEST SCENE

Four lines, 28 words:

ANTONY
Set our squadrons on yon side o' the hill,
In eye of Caesar's battle; from which place
We may the number of the ships behold,
And so proceed accordingly.

Antony and Cleopatra, Act III, scene ix

THE LONGEST SCENE

920 lines, 7137 words:

Love's Labour's Lost, Act V, scene ii
(I won't reproduce it here!)

Worst Body Odour

Caliban in **The Tempest** and Cloten in **Cymbeline** vie for the
honour of being the smelliest character in Shakespeare.

In **Cymbeline** Cloten exerts himself in a sword fight, making him
'reek like a sacrifice'.

In **The Tempest** Trinculo, finding Caliban, says he 'smells like a
fish; a very ancient and fish-like smell; a kind of not-of-the-
newest poor-john: a strange fish'.

POTTED PLOTS

In which I reduce some of Shakespeare's masterpieces to a
paragraph...

Macbeth
Witches entertain themselves by making up cod prophecy of
kingship for Macbeth, a vicious Scottish warlord. Macbeth foolishly
tells trophy wife about possible kingship promotion; wife mocks
him; says he's weak when he says he'd rather 'Do the Right Thing'.
Macbeth cannot handle the mockery; murders current king; is
crowned. No longer trusts best mate so has him assassinated; sees
best mate's ghost; trophy wife goes mad, commits suicide; more
murders, loads of blood, gore and witches; Edward the Confessor
saves the day. Macbeth dies.

King Lear
Old King disinherits virtuous daughter while giving up his kingdom
to her two evil siblings; gets upset when said siblings stint on
hospitality to their aged parent; goes mad, rips off clothes, runs
amok on heathland during a thunderstorm, howls at moon.
Meanwhile Duke of Gloucester has his eyes poked out by old king's
evil son-in-law. Virtuous daughter raises army; baddies eventually get
their respective comeuppances through stabbings, poison and sword
fights, but not before virtuous daughter (hanged) and king (broken
heart; old age) both die.

Hamlet

Hamlet, Prince of Denmark, communes with the ghost of his father, who unknown to everyone was murdered by Hamlet's uncle – now king – who is now married to his mother, the queen. Understandably upset, the prince plots his revenge – but feigns madness to deflect suspicion. Play climaxes with the death of the queen (poisoned chalice), the death of Ophelia's brother Laertes (stabbed by a poisoned rapier), the death of the king (stabbed by the poisoned rapier, forced to drink from the poisoned chalice) and the death of Hamlet (stabbed by the poisoned rapier, chooses to drink from the poisoned chalice). Horatio wants to die too; Hamlet won't let him. Fortinbras becomes king.

Henry IV Part II

Play opens with rumours of the death of Henry IV and Hal, his lackadaisical son (later of 'Once more unto the breach' and 'St Crispin's Day' fame). Rumour is wrong: the king returns to dreams of crusading in Jerusalem; Hal to the company of rotund ne'er-do-well Falstaff. Much Shakespearean innuendo and practical joking. This interrupted by the revolt of the Archbishop of York and the Duke of Northumberland. The king summons Hal, leaving Falstaff to travel to Gloucestershire to recruit soldiers to the king's cause. Further comic interludes. Yorkist army runs away after being foiled by cunning plan carried out by John, Hal's cold-hearted-but-dull younger brother. Hal returns to London, snatches crown off still-undead father, apologises, becomes king, then snubs Falstaff when he next bumps into him. Falstaff sent to prison by his arch-enemy, the Lord Chief Justice.

FEWEST LINES

Pity the actor playing the King of France's attendant in *All's Well That Ends Well* who has just four words for the entire play: 'I shall, my liege'. The same number of words goes to the Second Pirate in *Pericles, Prince of Tyre*: 'A prize! A prize!'

For the actor who plays Taurus in *Antony and Cleopatra*, the sum of his role comes to two words: 'My Lord', while the Fourth Soldier in Act IV, scene ii of *Julius Caesar* has nothing to say but: 'Stand!'

However, the shortest part of all goes to the Second Senator in *Cymbeline*, Act II, scene vii. He has a grand total of one word, consisting of just two letters: 'Ay'.

MEATIEST ROLES

Hamlet has the most lines in a single play with 1569 lines, followed by Richard III with 1151 lines. Iago has 1088 in Othello, while King Henry has 1031 in Henry V. Indeed Hal, later Henry V, with starring roles in no less than three plays, has the largest number of lines spoken by any character across Shakespeare's plays as a whole. He appears in Henry IV Part I and II and also in Henry V, and has 1915 lines. The character of Falstaff has the next meatiest role across more than one play, with 1681 lines, followed by Richard of Gloucester (later Richard III) with 1531 lines.

Female parts, in contrast, are much shorter, partly because in Shakespeare's theatre these roles were taken by young boy actors. Rosalind in As You Like It tops the table of largest speaking parts with just 685 lines, followed by Cleopatra in Antony and Cleopatra with 678 lines and Imogen in Cymbeline with 594 lines.

MOST DIFFICULT TO STAGE, PART I

It is not always easy to stage Shakespeare – indeed sometimes it seems the playwright goes out of his way to make things difficult for directors. *All's Well That Ends Well*, for example, has a notoriously problematic final scene in which Bertram instantaneously switches from loathing Helena his wife to loving her in the space of a single line. On discovering that she has tricked him into sleeping with her he relinquishes a whole play's worth of vitriol in a moment, promising to 'love her dearly, ever, ever dearly'.

Another notorious scene occurs in *The Winter's Tale*, after Antigonus is charged with the killing of Hermione's infant daughter. Here his abandoning of the baby on the shores of Bohemia is followed by the notoriously tricky stage direction of Act 3, scene iii: 'Exit, pursued by a bear.' An intriguing possibility is that a live animal was used in the original productions: bear-baiting was certainly a popular sport in the sixteenth and seventeenth centuries, and there were bear-baiting arenas in the vicinity of the Globe and Rose theatres. Modern directors, however, tend to opt for the actor-in-a-bear-suit solution to the dilemma.

Another late play, *Cymbeline*, has an equally problematic stage direction in Act 5, scene iv. Posthumus, wrongly gaoled for rebelling against the king and siding with the Romans, is visited in his sleep by the ghosts of his brothers, mother and father. Their appeal to Jupiter for justice is met with the following stage direction: 'Jupiter descends in thunder and lightning, sitting upon an eagle. He throws a thunderbolt.' After chastizing the ghosts for meddling in earthly affairs Jupiter ascends once more to the heavens. Again we have no idea how this would have been staged in Shakespeare's time.

MOST INAPPROPRIATE LOVE SCENE

In Act I, scene ii of *Richard III*, Richard wins the heart of Lady Anne, whose husband Edward, Prince of Wales, and father-in-law Henry VI he has just murdered. This wooing is all the more inappropriate in that it takes place over the corpse of the dead king.

In Act 1, scene ii we see Anne's initial hostility towards Richard melt in the face of some of the most eloquent and moving love poetry that Shakespeare ever wrote. While the audience might be amazed that Anne can so quickly forget her husband and his violent death, it can also marvel at Richard's ability so effortlessly to seduce the widow of a man he's just murdered:

DUKE OF GLOUCESTER
Your beauty ... did haunt me in my sleep
To undertake the death of all the world,
So I might live one hour in your sweet bosom.

LADY ANNE
If I thought that, I tell thee, homicide,
These nails should rend that beauty from my cheeks.

DUKE OF GLOUCESTER
These eyes could not endure that beauty's wreck;
You should not blemish it if I stood by:
As all the world is cheered by the sun,
So I by that; it is my day, my life.

Once Richard is left to himself, however, we see how utterly Machiavellian he is and how this eloquence is nothing more than camouflage for untrammelled ambition and double-dealing:

> Was ever woman in this humour woo'd?
> Was ever woman in this humour won?
> I'll have her; but I will not keep her long.
> What! I, that kill'd her husband and his father—
> To take her in her heart's extremest hate,
> With curses in her mouth, tears in her eyes,
> The bleeding witness of my hatred by;
> Having God, her conscience, and these bars
>   against me,
> And I no friends to back my suit at all,
> But the plain devil and dissembling looks,
> And yet to win her, all the world to nothing!
>   Ha!

Swords as Sweethearts

Even as Wild West gunslingers might have developed an affection for their six-shooters, Shakespearean swashbucklers can display an unhealthy attachment to their weapons. In *Henry IV, Part II*, faux swaggerer Pistol gently lays down his sword with the words: 'And, sweetheart, lie thou there!'

THE POWER OF EXCLAMATIONS – 'O! O! O!'

Poignant and moving in context, some of the exclamations uttered by Shakespeare's characters can sound a bit melodramatic taken outside their setting within the play. Hence Othello's cries of 'O! O! O!' as he falls on to the bed next to the corpse of the wife he's just strangled may underline the intensity of his grief within the play; outside of the play's context, though, it just sounds a bit silly.

From tragedy to comedy: the Nurse's reaction on hearing of the supposed death of Juliet in Act IV, scene v of *Romeo and Juliet* is probably as heartfelt as Othello's 'O! O! O!' – only potentially much funnier given her voluble, gossipy character. It is also full of dramatic irony, given the eventual tragic outcome of events.

> **O woe! O woeful, woeful, woeful day!**
> **Most lamentable day, most woeful day,**
> **That ever, ever, I did yet behold!**
> **O day! O day! O day! O hateful day!**
> **Never was seen so black a day as this:**
> **O woeful day, O woeful day!**

MOST DIFFICULT TO STAGE, PART II

It is not just the comedies and the 'problem plays' that offer staging dilemmas; the tragedies also have their own stock of difficulties.

The foremost of these in *Macbeth*, for example, is the march of Birnam Wood in Act V, scene iv. Here Malcolm's army chops down the branches of trees to disguise their numbers – thus fulfilling the witches' prophecy of Macbeth's downfall: 'Fear not till Birnam Wood/Do come to Dunsinane'. The second staging dilemma occurs in the final scene in the play, when Macduff enters 'with Macbeth's head'. Papier-mâché historians relate that 'japanning', the art of producing solid objects from mashed-up paper, only reached England in the mid-seventeenth century – so we can only imagine how Shakespearean prop managers would have dealt with this particular stage direction.

Another interesting and supremely gory staging challenge involves the putting out of the Earl of Gloucester's eyes in *King Lear*, Act 3, scene vii. This challenge is made all the greater by the fact that the earl has three acts of the play after his eyes have been put out to wander, blinded and bloodied, as the tragedy unfolds.

However, Shakespeare's supreme gore-fest *Titus Andronicus* has to be the winner in the most-difficult-to-stage stakes. A single stage direction in Act II, scene iv causes all the problems:

'Enter the Empress's sons with Lavinia, her hands cut off, and her tongue cut out, and ravished.'

For the remainder of the play a mute, blood-spattered, deranged Lavinia staggers across the stage, her suffering a silent witness to the cruelty of Aaron, the empress and her sons. Indeed so difficult is this scene to stage that modern directors have often attempted more stylised or abstract stagings, replacing the blood with ribbons, for example, or absenting Lavinia from the action altogether. Sometimes, it seems, even Shakespeare may go too far.

2
ELIZABETHANS
BEHAVING BADLY

ANTI-SOCIAL BEHAVIOUR

The anti-social behaviour of teenagers is hardly new, it seems.
In *The Winter's Tale*, a shepherd has it about right when he
observes in Act III, scene ii:

> I would there were no age between ten and three-and-
> twenty, or that youth would sleep out the rest; for there is
> nothing in the between but getting wenches with child,
> wronging the ancientry, stealing, fighting.

Not much change there then.

BINGE DRINKING

Shakespeare's plays are full of drunks, and he has a lot to say on the subject of drinking to excess. In *Othello*, for example, Iago deliberately gets Cassio drunk, knowing that if he does so Cassio will be liable to get involved in a brawl and thus incur Othello's displeasure. In the event Cassio proves to be the worst kind of drunk: quarrelsome and obnoxious, he ends up striking Roderigo and wounding Montano. In the meantime Iago philosophises on the relative merits of the English, Danish, German and Dutch when they are drunk. He states the English are the 'most potent in potting' because an Englishman can 'drink with facility your Dane dead drunk; he sweats not to overthrow your Almaine; he gives your Hollander a vomit, 'ere the next pottle can be filled'.

In *Twelfth Night* the appropriately named Sir Toby Belch spends much of the play reeling across the stage in a joyously drunken stupor. Feste, the clown, comments that a drunken man is 'like a drown'd man, a fool, and a madman/One draught above heat makes him a fool, the second mads him, and a third drowns him'.

Other notable drunks are the porter in *Macbeth*, Stephano, Trinculo and Caliban in *The Tempest* – and, of course, Falstaff and his roguish companions in *Henry IV Parts I* and *II* and *Henry V*. But perhaps the luckiest drunk is Barnardine in *Measure for Measure*, whose execution is stayed because he is too drunk to provide consent for it.

'YOUR MUM'

The best example of a 'your mum'-type insult in Shakespeare is in Act IV, scene ii of Titus Andronicus, where Aaron exclaims:

'I have done your mother.'

He means exactly what he says.

Good in Bed?

Is Cleopatra the best shag in Shakespeare? She might be if Enobarbus is to be believed. In Act 2, scene ii Maecenas points out the necessity of Antony leaving Cleopatra for Caesar's sister Octavia. Enobarbus explains why it will simply not happen:

> **Never! He will not.**
> **Age cannot wither her, nor custom stale**
> **Her infinite variety. Other women cloy**
> **The appetites they feed: but she makes hungry**
> **Where most she satisfies.**

OBSCENE GESTURES

Much has been made of the thumb-biting scene at the start of
Romeo and Juliet where Samson, spying two followers of the house of
Montague, declares: 'I will bite my thumb at them;/Which is a
disgrace to them, if they bear it.' Rude as the gesture was to an
Elizabethan audience, there is at least one other very obscene gesture
in Shakespeare with a history and explanation at least as interesting
as thumb-biting: the Fig of Spain.

The following exchange in *Henry V*, Act III, scene iv is just one of a
number of instances in which Pistol's fiery temperament finds a
physical expression in the Fig of Spain:

> **FLUELLEN**
> **It is well.**
>
> **PISTOL**
> **The fig of Spain!**

Here Pistol's words would have been accompanied with the actor
thrusting his thumb between his middle and index fingers, the
symbolism being relatively easy to work out (try it yourself).

Shakespearean audiences may or may not have known that the
gesture dates back at least to the time of ancient Rome, where it was
known as the *mano fico*. Here *mano* translates as 'hand' and *fico* as 'fig'
– which may possibly be a play on the Latin word *fica*, a slang term
referring to the female vulva.

MISOGYNY, PART I

A lot of it about in Shakespeare, but perhaps the most savage
example of misogyny falls from the deranged mind of King Lear
when meditating on the unnatural lusts of his less than kind
elder daughters:

> **Down from the waist they are centaurs,**
> **Though women all above;**
> **But to the girdle do the gods inherit,**
> **Beneath is all the fiends' –**
> **There's hell, there's darkness, there is the sulphurous pit –**
> **Burning, scalding, stench, consumption.**
> **Fie, fie, fie! Pah, pah!**
>
> Act 4, scene vi

OBESITY

In *The Comedy of Errors* Dromio of Syracuse discovers that Nell, an overweight kitchen maid, has been lusting after him. He describes her as 'spherical, like a globe', adding 'I could find out countries in her'. He says that Ireland is 'in her buttocks' and that he 'found it out by the bogs'.

In *Henry IV, Part I* Mistress Quickly describes how Falstaff has eaten her 'out of house and home' and how he has 'put all my substance into that fat belly of his'. Later in the same play Hal describes Falstaff as a 'fat villain', while Doll Tearsheet likens him to 'a hulk … stuffed in the hold'.

Dr Johnson probably has the best line when describing Falstaff's rotundity, however. He called him a 'swollen excrescence of a man'.

What's Eating Iago?

Iago in *Othello* has to be one of Shakespeare's nastiest characters. He dupes Roderigo out of his wealth, ruins Cassio's good name, stabs his own wife literally in the back and works Othello up into such a froth of jealous rage that he kills the utterly blameless Desdemona.

Critics have long been split about what exactly motivates Iago to act with such spite towards all those around him. There are, however, hints within the play – especially about his loathing of Othello. In Act I, scene iii he says he hates Othello because of rumours that the Moor has committed adultery with his wife, Emilia: 'And it is thought abroad that 'twixt my sheets /He's done my office.' The same theme appears in Iago's conversation with Roderigo in Act 2, when he declares:

> ... I do suspect the lustful Moor
> Hath leap'd into my seat; the thought whereof
> Doth like a poisonous mineral gnaw my inwards;
> And nothing can nor shall content my soul
> Till I am even'd with him...
>
> Act 2, scene i

ALL MEN ARE BASTARDS

At least that's what seems to be implied by Balthazar's song in Act II, scene iii of *Much Ado About Nothing*:

> **Sigh no more, ladies, sigh no more,**
> **Men were deceivers ever, –**
> **One foot in sea and one on shore,**
> **To one thing constant never.**

In *Cymbeline* Posthumus Leonatus comes to the same conclusion – 'We [men] are all bastards' – but for totally different reasons. His conclusion is that all men are essentially bastards because of the infidelity of their mothers.

MISOGYNY, PART II

Like King Lear, *Cymbeline*'s Posthumus Leonatus has a profoundly jaundiced view of women. After being duped into believing his wife Imogen has been unfaithful with the dastardly Iachimo, he ascribes to women faults such as 'lying', 'flattering', 'lust and rank thoughts', 'revenges', 'ambitions', 'covetings', 'changes of prides', 'disdain', 'nice longing', 'slanders' and 'mutability'. He adds:

> **All faults that may be named, nay, that hell knows,**
> **Why, hers, in part or all; but rather, all.**

WAS SHAKESPEARE A RACIST?

It is not pleasant and should not be sugar-coated, but racism is hard to avoid in Shakespeare. Critics point out that Shakespeare's empathy with the persecuted in plays such as *Othello* and *The Merchant of Venice* actually provides insight into how corrosive racism is – and that this insight therefore ultimately carries an anti-racist message. At the same time it's hard to get away from the fact that a contemporary Shakespearean audience would have been far removed from any modern multi-cultural mindset, and would probably have had little empathy for any 'outsiders' in the plays.

Regardless of how you interpret its meaning or intent, however, racism crops up most explicitly in *Othello*, *The Merchant of Venice*, *Titus Andronicus* and *The Tempest*.

Othello

In *Othello* the central character, a Moor of African descent, is defined by his skin colour: in the eyes of his enemies it – and a beast-like lust – become his defining characteristics. In Iago's words he is a 'black ram' responsible for 'tupping [Brabantio's] white ewe'; he is also described as a 'Barbary horse', 'the thick lips' and 'a devil'.

According to one reading it is Othello's status as an outsider that makes him so susceptible to Iago's machinations. In one key passage, where he first plants the seeds of doubt about Desdemona's fidelity in Othello's mind, Iago deftly plays on the Moor's ignorance of, and insecurity about, Venetian society:

> I know our country disposition well:
> In Venice [wives] do let God see the pranks
> They dare not show their husbands; their
> best conscience
> Is not to leave't undone, but keep't unknown.

Act 3, scene iii

The Merchant of Venice

The Merchant of Venice is another play that for modern audiences has a problematic attitude towards race. Here, in common with the character of Othello, Shylock is first and foremost an outsider. In the court scene at the play's culmination, for example, he is referred by his name just six times and as 'Jew' a full 22 times. The audience is left in little doubt that it is partly his Jewishness that drives his desire for revenge against Antonio and his 'pound of flesh'. Anyone 'worth the name of a Christian', it is implied, would have opted for a far more reasonable arrangement.

Titus Andronicus and *The Tempest*

In Act IV, scene ii of *Titus Andronicus* Aaron, a Moor, fathers an illegitimate son who is described by its nurse as 'A joyless, dismal, black and sorrowful issue' and 'as loathsome as a toad'. The child's mother, the empress, fearful that the emperor will discover her infidelity, persuades the nurse to tell Aaron to 'christen [the child] with thy dagger's point' (ie to murder it). Aaron resists, however, declaring:

> **Zounds, ye whore! Is black so base a hue?**
> **Sweet blowse, you are a beauteous blossom, sure.**

Later in the same scene Aaron decides to deliver a passionate defence of his blackness:

> **Coal-black is better than another hue,**
> **In that it scorns to bear another hue...**

In *The Tempest*, meanwhile, Caliban is described as 'this thing of darkness'. Throughout the play he remains an outsider, a malignant force, because of his 'deformity' and skin colour.

Racist language also crops up in *Love's Labour's Lost* (Act 4, scene iii), in which Ferdinand, King of Navarre, declares that

> **Black is the badge of hell**
> **The hue of dungeons and the scowl of night.**

Likewise in Act II, scene v of *The Two Gentlemen of Verona* Launce tells Speed:

> **If thou wilt, go with me to an alehouse; if not,**
> **thou are a Hebrew, a Jew, and not worth the**
> **name of a Christian.**

Richard II, *Henry IV Part II*, *Antony and Cleopatra*, *The Merry Wives of Windsor*, *Much Ado About Nothing* and *Macbeth* also have examples of racist language.

What's Eating Shylock?

Of all of Shakespeare's characters Shylock has to win first prize for avarice – and this vice can be considered to be one of the driving forces for his general nastiness throughout the play. When his daughter elopes with Lorenzo – carrying off his stock of gold and jewellery in the process – his first concern is not for the loss of his daughter's love, but for the loss of his material wealth. His mixed-up priorities find expression with the following: 'I would my daughter were dead at my foot, and the ducats in her coffin!' Earlier in the play Solanio mocks Shylock's confused reaction to the loss of his daughter and his gold:

> **As the dog Jew did utter in the streets:**
> **'My daughter! – O my ducats! – O my daughter!**
> **Fled with a Christian! – O my Christian ducats! –**
> **Justice! the law! My ducats and my daughter!'**
>
> *Act 2, scene* viii

INCEST, PART I

Yes, even incest has its place in Shakespeare. Not content with littering his plays with beheadings, hangings, poisonings, drownings and stabbings, the Bard also chooses plots in which some of his characters partake of some pretty dubious sexual shenanigans. In *Pericles* Antiochus, the king of Antioch, is engaged in a secret incestuous relationship with his daughter. Pericles guesses what is happening and flees the country before Antiochus can have him put to death for fear of his revealing the secret.

Pericles describes how the king 'with foul incest' partakes of 'actions blacker than night':

> **Where now you're both a father and a son,**
> **By your untimely claspings with your child**
> **(Which pleasure fits a husband, not a father);**
> **And she an eater of her mother's flesh**
> **By the defiling of her parent's bed;**
> **And both like serpents are...**

Act 1, scene i

Eventually father and daughter get their just deserts, of course: both are struck and killed by lightning.

INCEST, PART II

In *Hamlet*, there is more than just a suggestion that Claudius's relationship with Gertrude is incestuous as he is the brother of her dead husband. That a Shakespearean audience would have found such a union offensive is clear from the 1563 *Table of Kindred and Affinity*, which describes how people related to one another – even through wedlock – were forbidden 'in scripture and [the] laws' from marrying. Thus it is that the king's description of his new wife – whom he has married barely a month after murdering her husband – as 'sometime sister, now our queen' would have been considered especially distasteful. The same moral – and physical – revulsion lies behind Hamlet's lament for his mother's eagerness to be bedded by the king in 'incestuous sheets'. The ghost, meanwhile, characterises Claudius as 'that incestuous, that adulterate beast' and warns his son to 'Let not the royal bed of Denmark be/A couch for luxury and damned incest'.

At the same time twentieth-century critics especially have been quick to point out that there is more than a hint of an Oedipus complex in Hamlet's speech in the famous scene (Act 3, scene iv) where he confronts his mother. Freud's *The Interpretation of Dreams*, published in 1900, led the way with a view that Hamlet has an 'Oedipal desire for his mother and the subsequent guilt [prevents] him from murdering [Claudius], who has done what he unconsciously wanted to do'.

3
SUBVERSIVE SHAKESPEARE

EUPHEMISMS IN SHAKESPEARE

Euphemisms abound in Shakespeare, their difficulty and abundance providing scholars and academics more than ample scope to mine the Bard's seamier side. Here are just a few of them.

'Peculiar river'
The phrase comes from Act I, scene ii of Measure for Measure where Claudio is sent to prison for 'getting Madam Julietta with child'. Mistress Overdone explains the situation to Pompey: Claudio is being punished as a result of 'Groping for trouts in a peculiar river'.

'Box unseen'
In Act II, scene iii of All's Well That Ends Well, Parolles urges Bertram to take up arms. The alternative is to wear out his 'honour' in a 'box unseen', 'spending' (i.e. ejaculating) his 'manly marrow'.

'Sweet nothings'

Much Ado About Nothing takes on an entirely different meaning if
we bear in mind that 'nothing' was Elizabethan slang for female
genitalia. A lot of wordplay occurs throughout Shakespeare on this
theme. As an example, take Hamlet's exchange with Ophelia at the
beginning of the 'play within a play' at the start of Act III, scene ii:

> **HAMLET**
> Lady, shall I lie ... my head upon your lap?

> **OPHELIA**
> Ay, my lord.

> **HAMLET**
> Do you think I meant country matters?

> **OPHELIA**
> I think nothing, my lord.

> **HAMLET**
> That's a fair thought to lie between maids' legs.

> **OPHELIA**
> What is, my lord?

> **HAMLET**
> Nothing.

'Cod's head and salmon's tail'

In Act II, scene i of Othello, Iago utters the following:

> **She that in wisdom never was so frail**
> **To change the cod's head for the salmon's tail…**

This pun's exact meaning is unclear, but the cod's head refers to a codpiece and the salmon's tail to female sexual parts.

'Velvet leaves'

In the following extract from Act I, scene iii of Love's Labour's Lost, the phrase 'velvet leaves' appears to be another euphemism:

> **Love, whose month is ever May,**
> **Spied a blossom passing fair**
> **Playing in the wanton air**
> **Through the velvet leaves the wind,**
> **All unseen, can passage find;**
> **That the lover, sick to death,**
> **Wish himself the heaven's breath.**

Here the wind finds a way to 'triumph' by passing through the velvet leaves – something to which the sick lover can only aspire.

'Bird's nest'

In Act II, scene v of Romeo and Juliet, the nurse promises her charge, the young Juliet Capulet, that to help her meet Romeo she will:

> **Fetch a ladder, by the which your love**
> **Must climb a bird's nest soon when it is dark...**

Scholars of sixteenth-century bawdiness relate that the bird's nest in question carries connotations not only of pubic hair and female genitalia, but also of fertility in the form of the new life it contains.

'Potato finger'

It may be very hard to believe nowadays, but in the sixteenth century the then-exotic potato was considered an aphrodisiac. This is perhaps the explanation of Falstaff's 'Let the sky rain potatoes' at his secret assignation with Mistresses Ford and Page in Act V, scene v of The Merry Wives of Windsor. Likewise, in Act V, scene ii of Troilus and Cressida, Thersites spies the heroine of the play dallying with Diomedes and exclaims: 'How the devil Luxury, with his fat rump and potato finger, tickles these together. Fry, lechery, fry!' In this case 'potato finger' is a euphemism for the male member.

THE ACT OF DARKNESS – BAD SEX IN SHAKESPEARE

There is a lot of sex in Shakespeare, though it is not always visible. His characters often use animal imagery to emphasise their disgust at the sexual act. In **Cymbeline** Posthumus Leonatus believes that Iachimo has seduced his wife Imogen and:

> **Like a full-acorn'd boar, a German one,**
> **Cried 'O!' and mounted.**

Act 2, scene v

In **Othello** Iago describes sex as 'making the beast with two backs'. Later in the play Othello relates how he believes Cassio and Desdemona 'hath the act of shame/A thousand times committed'.

In **King Lear** Edgar, disguised as Poor Tom, describes how in a previous life he had 'served the lust of [his] mistress's heart and did the act of darkness with her'.

More comically Falstaff, disguised as Herne the Hunter in **The Merry Wives of Windsor**, describes how love 'in some respects, makes a beast a man; in some other, a man a beast'. Which side of the fence Falstaff falls on when it comes to loving becomes clear as he observes:

> **For me, I am here a Windsor stag; and the fattest, I think,**
> **i' the forest. Send me a cool rut-time, Jove, or who can**
> **blame me to piss my tallow?**

Act 5, scene v

What's Eating Edmund?

Dashing but entirely lacking in moral scruples, Edmund in *King Lear* is the archetypal philanderer; his credentials in debauchery are unparalleled by any other character in Shakespeare. Not only does he seduce two high-born duchesses, daughters of the king himself, but the ladies themselves are sisters. On hearing about the suicide of Goneril and the poisoning of Regan, Edmund even appears to hint at the potential for a diabolical post-death *ménage à trois*: 'I was contracted to them both. All three/Now marry in an instant.'

In the play Edmund's wickedness seems to be driven firstly by the fact of his illegitimacy, but also by a lust for power. Even his deathbed repentance in the final scene goes against the grain of an innately evil character, as he himself admits:

> **I pant for life; some good I mean to do**
> **Despite of mine own nature.**
>
> *Act 5, scene iii*

DISGUISES

So many of Shakespeare's plots are constructed around the use of disguises to conceal identity that it is hard to know where to begin.

In **Measure for Measure** the Duke disguises himself as a friar so he can spy on Angelo. He only reveals his true identity after the full extent of Angelo's skulduggery has been revealed.

In **Cymbeline** Iachimo dresses up in Leonatus's clothes, making Imogen believe her husband has been killed when she finds his decapitated body. Later in the same play Leonatus disguises himself as a Roman soldier in the hope of dying on the battlefield.

In **Henry IV, Part I** Hal and Poins disguise themselves in suits of buckram (coarse linen) to rob Falstaff.

In **The Merry Wives of Windsor** it is Falstaff who turns up in disguise: in this instance Mistress Ford and Mistress Page gull him into dressing up first as a fat witch and then as Herne the Hunter. His reward in both cases is a sound beating.

In **Henry V** the king conceals his identity ahead of the Battle of Agincourt, fooling Pistol into thinking he is Harry Le Roy, an infantryman and 'a gentleman of a company'.

Perhaps the most interesting disguise of all, however, is that of Poor Tom in **King Lear**. Here Edgar, who has been wrongly accused of plotting against his father, disguises himself to 'take the basest and most poorest shape/that ever penury.../Brought near to beast'. Transformed as 'Poor Tom' he spends much of Acts II, III and IV masquerading as a mad beggar, talking gibberish to imaginary demons. He takes his cue from the 'Bedlam beggars' he has seen who put 'pins, wooden pricks, nails, sprigs of rosemary' in their 'numbed and mortified bare arms' with the object of eliciting sympathy and charity from passers-by. Actors playing Edgar have been known to take these stage directions literally – making for a painfully realistic interpretation of the Poor Tom character.

SHAKESPEAREAN FILTH – MORE EUPHEMISMS

'Dearest bodily part'
This comes from Act I, scene iv of *Cymbeline*, where the evil Iachimo lays a bet with Posthumus that he will 'enjoy ... the dearest bodily part of [his] mistress', Imogen.

'Flashing fire'
In Act II, scene i of *Henry V*, Pistol's fighting talk contains the following: 'Pistol's cock is up,/And flashing fire will follow.' This sort of euphemistic wordplay on Pistol's name occurs throughout Parts I and II of *Henry IV* and in *Henry V*.

'Hanging bugles in an invisible baldric'
To hang one's bugle in an invisible baldric is one of the more complicated of Shakespeare's innuendos and much scholarly ink has been spilled debating the meaning of this particular phrase as a result. It appears in Benedick's speech in Act I, scene i of *Much Ado About Nothing* in which he vows to remain a bachelor:

> **That a woman conceived me, I thank her; that she brought me up, I likewise give her most humble thanks: but that I will have a recheat winded in my forehead, or hang my bugle in an invisible baldrick, all women shall pardon me.**

Here a 'recheat' is a call from a hunting horn (horns of any kind had an indelible association with sex in the Elizabethan mindset). To have it 'winded' on your forehead would be to grow cuckold's horns, i.e. to have an unfaithful wife or lover. The bugle could be a euphemism for the male member, while a baldric is a belt for hanging a bugle, which here can be taken to be that hardy perennial of Elizabethan fashion, the codpiece. One reading then is that Benedick refuses to be cowed into making his manhood (bugle) inconspicuous by hiding it in an unostentatious codpiece (baldric).

Feeling horny

The Forester's song in Act IV, scene ii of *As You Like It* contains the following lines:

> **Take thou no scorn to wear the horn...**
> **Thy father's father wore it; And thy father bore it.**
> **The horn, the horn, the lusty horn,**
> **Is not a thing to laugh to scorn.**

Here the reference is not only to the cuckold's horns, but also to male genitalia.

Three-inch fool

Size matters, at least if Grumio is to be believed in Act IV, scene i of *The Taming of the Shrew*. Here he responds to Curtis's 'Away, you three-inch fool!' with the following (note, yet again, the reference to cuckold's horns):

> **Am I but three inches? Why, thy horn is a foot, and so long**
> **am I at the least.**

'Pizzle'

Falstaff in *Henry IV, Part I*, on learning of the plot by Hal and Poins to rob him, utters some splendidly filthy invective with more than one euphemistic reference to male genitalia:

> **'Sblood, you starveling, you eel-skin, you dried neat's-tongue, you bull's pizzle, you stock-fish! – O for breath to utter what is like thee! – you tailor's yard, you sheath, you bow-case; you vile standing tuck!**

> *Act 2, scene iv*

GROSS GOURMETS, PART I

In *King Lear* Edgar assumes the disguise of the mad vagabond Poor Tom. He describes his diet, which seems to consist largely of live amphibians, lizards, cow dung, rats, dead dogs and pond scum, in Act III, scene iv. Below is a list of his favourite morsels:

'the swimming frog'
'the toad'
'the todpole' (tadpole)
'the wall-newt' (lizard)
'cow dung for sallets' (cow dung as a side salad)
'old rat' (swallowed whole)
'ditch dog' (a dead dog thrown into a ditch)
'green mantle of the standing pool' (scum on a stagnant pond)

GENDER BENDERS

Gender play figures large in Shakespeare. This is perhaps
unsurprising given the ban on actresses on the Elizabethan stage:
the inversion of traditional male and female roles was almost a given
within the notoriously racy confines of the playhouse.

In *As You Like It* Rosalind disguises herself as 'Ganymede', while
her companion Celia takes on the disguise of 'Aliena'. As an example
of gender confusion in Shakespeare, Ganymede's mock wooing by
her pretended suitor Orlando at the end of Act IV is hard to beat.
Theatregoers would have been presented with a boy actor
pretending to be a woman, pretending to be a man, pretending to
be a woman, being wooed by a man superficially unaware that the
boy he is pretending to woo is a boy pretending to be a woman
pretending to be a man pretending to be a woman!

As You Like It is not the only play to rely on gender ambiguity to
drive its plot. In **Twelfth Night** Viola disguises herself as a male page,
Cesario. Here Shakespeare's audience would have been treated to a
triple irony as Viola (boy actor dressed as a woman dressed as a
man) falls in love with Orsino and in turn becomes the object of
Olivia's affections. As in so many of Shakespeare's comedies, resolution
is finally achieved only through the marriage of the protagonists:
Viola to Duke Orsino and Lady Olivia to Viola's twin brother Sebastian.

In **The Two Gentlemen of Verona** Julia and her maid Lucetta travel to
Milan disguised as men in pursuit of Julia's erstwhile lover Proteus.
Still in disguise, Julia contrives to be hired as Proteus's page.
Only a fainting fit and the recognition of a love token in the form
of a ring given to her by Proteus reveals her identity and duly
reconciles the two lovers.

COLDEST WORDS IN SHAKESPEARE

'I know thee not, old man.'

The words are spoken by Hal to Falstaff on their first meeting after Hal's coronation as Henry V. The new king casts off any associations with his one-time boon buddy and the world he inhabits, making it clear that Falstaff should:

> **Presume not that I am the thing I was,**
> **For God doth know, so shall the world perceive,**
> **That I have turn'd away my former self;**
> **So will I those that kept me company.**
>
> *Act 5, scene v*

The affection that Falstaff arouses in audiences renders his rejection by Hal cruel and distressing, even while we appreciate rationally that it is inevitable, and even the correct course for the new king.

SADDEST WORDS IN SHAKESPEARE

For lovers of Falstaff, Shakespeare's larger-than-life lecherer, drinker and loveable rogue, the following might just qualify as the saddest words in Shakespeare:

Master Shallow, I owe you a thousand pound.

Act 5, scene v

The line is spoken by a crestfallen Falstaff to Justice Shallow, from whom he has borrowed on the expectation of preferment under Hal, straight after he has been rejected by the new king. So great has Falstaff's life-affirming power been, despite his degenerate way of life, that we feel his defeat as an almost physical shock.

This is literally the first and only time in any of the plays that we see the hitherto untouchable Falstaff at a loss for words and utterly impotent in the face of a setback. Significantly it is also the only time we ever see him admitting to owing someone else money; in all other instances he has attempted to bamboozle his creditors. The play ends with a sadder, feebler Falstaff being thrown into the Fleet Prison by his nemesis, the Lord Chief Justice, preparing the way for his death in *Henry V*.

4
THE FINAL
FRONTIER

SHAKESPEARE IN SPACE

Twenty-four of Uranus's 27 moons are named after characters in Shakespeare's plays. The discoverer of Uranus, the eighteenth-century English astronomer William Herschel, proposed that the planet be named 'Georgium Sidus' ('George's Star') after King George III, since it was the first planet discovered by an Englishman. In the event, however, the scientific community opted to continue in the classical tradition of naming planets. They eventually plumped for Uranus, the ancient Greek deity of the sky, on the suggestion of German astronomer Johann Elert Bode.

In 1787, six years after announcing his discovery of Uranus, Herschel observed two moons in orbit around the planet. This time Herschel got his way, despite continued protests from outside England, and took his names from a play by England's acknowledged national poet. He decided to name the moons Titania and Oberon after the King and Queen of the Fairies in *A Midsummer Night's Dream*. When another English astronomer, William Lassell, discovered a further two large moons in Uranus's orbit in 1851 he decided to continue with Herschel's idea of using characters from English literary works, naming the two new bodies Ariel and Umbriel from Alexander Pope's celebrated poem *The Rape of the Lock*. Later discoveries reverted to Shakespearean characters, and now 13 of his plays are represented among Uranus's moons.

Cordelia
The only virtuous daughter in *King Lear*

Ophelia
The daughter of Polonius in *Hamlet*

Bianca
Sister of Katherine in *The Taming of the Shrew*

Cressida
The title character in *Troilus and Cressida*

Desdemona
Othello's faithful wife in *Othello*

Juliet
Juliet Capulet, the title character in *Romeo and Juliet*

Portia
Shylock's daughter in *The Merchant of Venice*

Rosalind
Heroine of *As You Like It*, daughter of banished Duke Senior

Mab
Not actually a character in any play, but Queen Mab is referred to in *Romeo and Juliet* – when Mercutio mocks Romeo for his listlessness brought on by an unrequited love for Rosaline:

> **O, then, I see Queen Mab hath been with you.**
> **She is the fairies' midwife, and she comes**
> **In shape no bigger than an agate stone**
> **On the fore-finger of an alderman,**
> **Drawn with a team of little atomies**
> **Athwart men's noses as they lie asleep.**
> *Act 1, scene iv*

'Queen Mab' is also the title of a poem by Percy Bysshe Shelley, so Mab could be considered one of the moons not named after a Shakespearean character.

10 Belinda

Another non-Shakespearean character, Belinda is a character in Alexander Pope's mock-heroic epic poem *The Rape of the Lock*.

11 Perdita

The daughter cast away by Leontes in *The Winter's Tale*

12 Puck

The impish servant of Oberon in *A Midsummer Night's Dream*

13 Cupid

Features in Sonnet 153 and in *Timon of Athens*

14 Miranda

Prospero's daughter in *The Tempest*

15 Francisco

One of the retinue of Alonso, King of Naples, in *The Tempest*

16 Ariel

The spirit servant of Prospero in *The Tempest*, but also a character in Pope's *The Rape of the Lock*. We know that Ariel, the moon, was discovered at the same time as Umbriel, so it is most probable that both are named after the characters in Pope's poem rather than just one after a Shakespearean character.

17 **Umbriel**
From Pope's *The Rape of the Lock*

18 **Titania**
Queen of the Fairies in *A Midsummer Night's Dream*

19 **Oberon**
King of the Fairies in *A Midsummer Night's Dream*

20 **Caliban**
Son of the witch Sycorax and Prospero's deformed slave
in *The Tempest*

21 **Stephano**
A drunken butler in *The Tempest*

22 **Trinculo**
A jester, Stephano's sidekick in *The Tempest*

23 **Sycorax**
A witch and Caliban's mother in *The Tempest*

24 **Margaret**
A maid in *Much Ado About Nothing*

Prospero

Magician and father of Miranda in The Tempest

Setebos

The name of the god worshipped by the witch Sycorax in The Tempest. Interestingly Setebos was one of the gods worshipped by the Patagonians, and has been cited as one of many clues locating the island where the action in The Tempest takes place. It is thought to be somewhere off the South American mainland.

Ferdinand

The son of Alonso, King of Naples in The Tempest

SHAKESPEARE ON TV

The BBC's 'Complete Dramatic Works of William Shakespeare', released between 1978 and 1985, is probably the most comprehensive small-screen rendering of the Bard's output. It includes a version of every single play from the established canon.

Notable performances included Helen Mirren as Rosalind in *As You Like It* (1979), Anthony Quayle as Falstaff in *Henry IV, Part II* (1979) and Anthony Hopkins as *Othello* (1980).

More out of the ordinary was the casting of Roger Daltrey as the Dromio twins in *The Comedy of Errors* (1983) and John Cleese as Petruchio in *The Taming of the Shrew* (1980).

SHOOTING SHAKESPEARE – THE BARD AT THE MOVIES

So many different versions of Shakespeare have appeared on either the small screen or in the cinema that there is easily enough material for a book in itself.

King John, produced by Sir Herbert Beerbohm-Tree in 1899, is generally held to be the first film adaptation of a Shakespeare play. Since then there have been literally hundreds of Shakespeare movies – both faithful reproductions and versions loosely based on the original plays or using them as the starting point for new departures. Here are just a few of the acknowledged leviathans of Shakespeare on the silver screen:

Laurence Olivier
Quite aside from living and breathing Shakespeare in an infinite variety of stage productions, Olivier starred in and directed definitive versions of Henry V (1944), Hamlet (1948) and Richard III (1955). A true titan of Shakespeare at the movies.

Orson Welles
Directed a 1948 version of Macbeth; directed Othello and played the role in a 1952 version of the play. Directed and played Falstaff in Chimes at Midnight (1967), which featured scenes from Richard II, Henry IV Part I, Henry IV Part II, Henry V and The Merry Wives of Windsor.

Akira Kurosawa

Best known for his virtuoso retellings in Japanese of the best-known tragedies. *The Bad Sleep Well* (*Warui Yatsu Hodo Yoku Nemuru*, 1960) is a quirky retelling of *Hamlet*, while *Ran* (1985) is a very loose adaptation of *King Lear*. Meanwhile, *The Throne of Blood* (*Kumonosu-jo*), also known as *The Castle of the Spider's Web*, 1957, is generally acknowledged to be the most accomplished foreign language version of *Macbeth*.

Roman Polanski

Polanski's 1971 gore-fest adaptation of *Macbeth* is notable not just for a nude sleep-walking scene featuring Francesca Annis, but also for its ultra-violent depiction of Duncan's assassination. A mountain of folklore has built up around Polanski's association with the Manson murders and its influence on the film.

Franco Zeffirelli

Another director whose name has become synonymous with classic on-screen takes of Shakespeare. His 1966 version of *The Taming of the Shrew*, in which Elizabeth Taylor and Richard Burton played Katherine and Petruchio, was followed up a year later with a box-office smash retelling of *Romeo and Juliet*, with Olivia Hussey and Leonard Whiting as Romeo and Juliet, Michael York as Tybalt, John McEnery as Mercutio and Pat Heywood as the Nurse. Another famous Zeffirelli foray into the Shakespeare canon was his 1990 production of *Hamlet* that boasted Mel Gibson in the lead role and Glenn Close as the ill-fated Queen Gertrude.

Kenneth Branagh

Branagh's Shakespeare credentials go far beyond any single acting or directorial role: he has been credited with reviving interest in Shakespeare as a cinematic experience.

In *Henry V* (director, 1989) he played Hal, alongside Ian Holm as Fluellen, Brian Blessed as Exeter and Emma Thompson as Katherine.

In an all-star version of *Much Ado About Nothing* (director, 1993) Branagh played Benedick, with Emma Thompson as Beatrice, Denzel Washington as Don Pedro, Robert Sean Leonard as Claudio, Kate Beckinsale as Hero, Michael Keaton as Dogberry and Keanu Reeves as the evil Don John.

Othello (1995) saw Branagh relinquish directorial control in favour of a masterful performance as an ingratiating and thoroughly untrustworthy Iago.

In 1996's four-hour *Hamlet*, Branagh as director is credited with the only totally unexpurgated version of the play on film. A loss of form in the widely panned musical rendition of *Love's Labour's Lost* (2000) was followed in 2006 by *As You Like It* with Kevin Kline as Jaques and Alfred Molina as Touchstone.

OTHER SHAKESPEAREANS ON FILM

Douglas Fairbanks
Petruchio, *The Taming of the Shrew* (1929)

James Cagney
Bottom, *A Midsummer Night's Dream* (1935)

Mickey Rooney
Puck, *A Midsummer Night's Dream* (1935)

Charlton Heston
Mark Antony, *Julius Caesar* (1949)
Mark Antony, *Julius Caesar* (1970)
Director, Antony, *Antony and Cleopatra* (1972)

Marlon Brando
Mark Antony, *Julius Caesar* (1953)

John Gielgud
Cassius, *Julius Caesar* (USA, 1953)
Clarence, *Richard III* (UK, 1955)
Henry IV, *Chimes at Midnight* (1967)
Caesar, *Julius Caesar* (USA, 1970)
Prospero, *Prospero's Books* (adaptation of *The Tempest*, 1991)

Leslie Nielsen
The Captain, *Forbidden Planet* (a classic sci-fi film loosely based on *The Tempest*, 1956)

Kenneth Williams
Caesar, *Carry On Cleo* (a very loose adaptation of *Antony and Cleopatra* and *Julius Caesar*, 1965)

Diana Rigg
Edwina Lionheart, *Theatre of Blood* (1973)

Derek Jarman
Director, *The Tempest* (1979)

Toyah Wilcox
Miranda, *The Tempest* (1979)

Molly Ringwald
Miranda, *The Tempest* (1982)
Cordelia, *King Lear* (a science-fiction adaptation of the play directed by Jean-Luc Godard, 1987)

Ben Kingsley
Feste, *Twelfth Night* (1996)

Helena Bonham-Carter
Olivia, *Twelfth Night* (1996)

Imogen Stubbs
Viola, *Twelfth Night* (1996)

Richard E. Grant
Sir Andrew Aguecheek, *Twelfth Night* (1996)

Anthony Hopkins

Titus Andronicus, *Titus Andronicus* (1999)

Heath Ledger

Patrick Verona, *10 Things I Hate about You*
(a loose adaptation of *The Taming of the Shrew*, 1999)

Michelle Pfeiffer

Titania, *A Midsummer Night's Dream* (1999)

Julia Stiles

Kat, *10 Things I Hate About You*
Desi, *O* (a modern adaptation of *Othello*, 2001)

Kevin Kline

Bottom, *A Midsummer Night's Dream* (1999)
Jaques, *As You Like It* (2006)

Al Pacino

Shylock, *The Merchant of Venice* (2004)

Jeremy Irons

Antonio, *The Merchant of Venice* (2004)

Helen Mirren

Prospera (a female version of Prospero), *The Tempest*, 2010

Michael Fassbender

Macbeth, *Macbeth*, 2015

SCIENCE FICTION

For some reason science fiction writers for television and film have a bit of a thing for using quotes from Shakespeare for their episode titles. *Star Trek* writers are probably the worst culprits, with episodes from both the original series and later spin-offs borrowing freely from Shakespeare for their titles.

Hamlet seems to have had the most profound influence on *Star Trek* writers, with at least four borrowings from the play used as titles. These include 'The Undiscovered Country' for one of the *Star Trek* movies (Act III, scene i); 'The Conscience of the King' for an episode from the original series (Act II, scene ii); 'Thine Own Self' for a *Star Trek: The Next Generation* episode (Act I, scene iii) and 'Mortal Coil' for a *Star Trek: Voyager* episode (Act III, scene i).

'The Dogs of War', the title of a *Star Trek: Deep Space Nine* episode, comes from Act III, scene i of *Julius Caesar*, while 'Dagger of the Mind' and 'All Our Yesterdays' for episodes of the original *Star Trek* come from *Macbeth*, Act II, scene i and Act V, scene v respectively. 'Once More Unto the Breach' for a *Star Trek: Deep Space Nine* episode comes from *Henry V*, Act III, scene I, while *King Lear* (Act I, scene iv) is the inspiration for the 'How Sharper Than A Serpent's Tooth' episode from the animated *Star Trek* series ('How sharper than a serpent's tooth it is to have a thankless child').

Shakespeare also provides the inspiration for two episodes of *Babylon 5*, another cult sci-fi series. One is entitled 'The Paragon of Animals' (from *Hamlet*, Act II, scene ii) and another 'The Quality of Mercy' (from *The Merchant of Venice*, Act II, scene ii).

Finally we return to *Star Trek* for the episode entitled 'By Any Other Name'. This well-known quote is from the famous balcony scene in

Act ii, scene ii of *Romeo and Juliet*: 'What's in a name? That which we call a rose/By any other name would still smell as sweet.'

Buffy, of vampire-slaying fame, has one of the books in the spin-off novels adapted from the television series using a Shakespeare quote for its title: '*The Evil that Men Do*'. The original is from the famous 'Friends, Romans, countrymen' speech in *Julius Caesar*, in which Mark Antony gives the funeral oration over the body of the dead emperor:

I come to bury Caesar, not to praise him.
The evil that men do lives after them,
The good is oft interred with their bones.

Act III, scene ii

Forbidden Planet, a 1956 sci-fi movie classic loosely based on *The Tempest*, includes Robby the Robot (who can be read either as a hi-tech re-rendering of Caliban or as an updated version of Ariel) and the Krell (who resemble Sycorax).

No discussion of Shakespeare in science fiction would be complete without mention of *Dr Who*, but this deserves a section to itself.

SHAKESPEARE AND THE TIME LORD

Dr Who aficionados know that the Time Lord's contact with the Bard goes way beyond 'The Shakespeare Code', the episode of the revived science-fiction series first aired on the BBC in 2007.

In 'The Chase', from 1965, the first Doctor, played by William Hartnell, and his companions gather round the Time Space Visualiser – a device that allows them to watch any event from any time and any place in history. Barbara Wright, played by Jacqueline Hill, chooses to watch an encounter between Elizabeth I and Shakespeare. They thus witness Elizabeth I providing the inspiration for *The Merry Wives of Windsor* and *Hamlet*.

In 'The Planet of Evil', first aired in 1975, Tom Baker plays the fourth Doctor and quotes from both *Hamlet* and *Romeo and Juliet*. He claims to have known the playwright before the start of his literary career. The plot for 'The Planet of Evil' takes its cue from *Forbidden Planet*, in turn based partly on *The Tempest*.

In 1979's 'City of Death' Tom Baker claims he helped Shakespeare to write *Hamlet* after the Bard injured his wrist writing sonnets.

In 'The Mark of the Rani', first aired in 1985, the sixth Doctor, played by Colin Baker, notes that he would like to meet up with Shakespeare again at some point.

In 'The Christmas Invasion' of 2005 David Tennant, in the role of the tenth Doctor, foils an invasion of Earth by the Sycorax. Here *The Tempest* is again the inspiration: Sycorax the witch is Caliban's mother.

The Doctor is also fond of quoting Shakespeare. In 'The Image of the Fendahl', first aired in 1977, Tom Baker addresses a skull with the phrase 'Alas, poor skull!' Likewise in 'The Two Doctors' (1985) Colin Baker says 'Good-night, sweet prince' to a dying colleague.

'The Shakespeare Code'

'The Shakespeare Code' is a 2007 episode of Dr Who that borrows heavily from Shakespeare for its storyline. Here the tenth Doctor, played by David Tennant, is accompanied by Martha Jones on her first trip in the Tardis as the Doctor's assistant. Their destination is Elizabethan England – and, naturally, one of the first things they do on arrival is to bump into Shakespeare, who is busily putting the finishing touches to a new play, *Love's Labour Won*. Unknown to them, however, the Carrionites – evil, witch-like aliens – aim to destroy the world by inserting a magical code into the closing words of the play.

As you would expect, the Doctor eventually saves the day – but not before much fun has been had by the writers of the episode with the concept of the Doctor interacting with the playwright. Among other things the Doctor is credited with the authorship of Sonnet 18 and inspires Shakespeare with the phrases 'All the world's a stage', 'The play's the thing', 'Once more unto the breach' and 'To be or not to be', all of which, of course, famously derive from the Shakespeare canon.

Interestingly the three Carrionites, who appear to be modelled on the Three Weird Sisters from *Macbeth*, use trochaic tetrameter and rhyming couplets for their spells, as do the witches in the original play.

BLACKADDER AND THE BARD

Classic BBC comedy series *Blackadder* paid its own unique homage to Shakespeare in 1999's 'Blackadder Back & Forth', in which Baldrick invents a time machine allowing Sir Edmund Blackadder to travel back to Elizabethan England. Bumping into Shakespeare in a corridor, Edmund first asks for his autograph, then knocks the Bard down with a single punch. He tells a nonplussed Shakespeare that the blow is on behalf of every schoolboy and schoolgirl for the next four hundred years:

> 'Have you any idea how much suffering you are going to cause? Hours spent at school desks trying to find one joke in A Midsummer Night's Dream. Years wearing stupid tights in school plays and saying things like "What ho, my lord" and "Oh, look, here comes Othello, talking total crap as usual".'

Later in the episode Edmund returns to England to find that things have been put out of joint by his escapades: Shakespeare is now only known as the inventor of the Biro. He has no choice but to go back in time once again and set things straight. This time, when he encounters Shakespeare, the following exchange takes place:

> Blackadder: I'm a very big fan, Bill.
> Shakespeare: Thank you.
> Blackadder: Keep up the good work. King Lear – very funny.

THE SIMPSONS

In 'Tales from the Public Domain', The Simpsons pays homage to Hamlet with Bart in the lead role. Moe plays Claudius, who marries Marge (as Gertrude) after poisoning King Hamlet (Homer). Homer returns as a ghost to incite Bart to revenge, while the famous 'play within a play' scene is helped along with the aid of Krusty the Clown. Bart (as Hamlet) accidentally kills Polonius (Chief Wiggum), after which his son Laertes (Ralph) challenges him to a duel.

True to the original, the story ends with a death-fest. Ralph, attempting a practice stab in his duel with Bart, kills himself, after which Bart kills Claudius. Carl and Lenny (playing Rosencarl and Guildenlenny) kill each other with poisoned high fives, while Bart dies after slipping on some blood. Marge kills herself with a mace after seeing how much mess there is to tidy up.

The Simpsons' second reference to Shakespeare came in Season 15 episode 'Co-Dependent's Day'. In the episode Moe slips up by giving away a priceless 1886 bottle of Chateau Latour. On discovering his mistake he bursts into tears – using a valuable original manuscript of Shakespeare's The Two Noble Kinsmen to dry his tears. It is possibly the widest airing the play has ever had: it is the only one of Shakespeare's plays that has never been adapted for television or film.

SOUTH PARK: 'SCOTT TENORMAN MUST DIE'

Episode 69 of the classic adult comedy animation series is loosely based on the plot of *Titus Andronicus*, Shakespeare's bloodiest play and a classic of the revenge tragedy genre.

In the *South Park* version Cartman cooks up an elaborate revenge on 15-year-old schoolboy Scott Tenorman who, among other things, has tricked him into paying $10 for a handful of his pubic hair. Cartman's revenge revolves around a wiener-eating pony, the band Radiohead and a chilli cook-off.

As in *Titus Andronicus*, the culmination of the revenge theme is a horrific, unintentional act of cannibalism involving a close family member. In Shakespeare's play Titus takes his revenge on the Empress Tamora by killing her sons Demetrius and Chiron, cooking them in a pie and then serving it up to her for dinner. In the *South Park* episode Cartman uses the hacked-up remains of Tenorman's parents as the ingredients for his chilli in the cook-off.

On discovering this the unfortunate Tenorman bursts into tears, prompting his favourite band, Radiohead, who have just appeared, to label him 'deeply uncool'. Cartman then licks Tenorman's tears and utters the immortal, almost Shakespearean lines: 'Ohhh, the tears of unfathomable sadness, mmm, yummy...yummy!' And: 'I made you eat your parents! I made you eat your parents!'

The episode was voted the most outrageous *South Park* episode by Comedy Central, the most popular episode by TV.com and the most rated episode by the Internet Movie Database.

CAPITALIZING ON THE BARD

Forget Hamlet Cigars: the commercialization of Shakespeare has scaled ever-greater heights since the advent of the internet.

The Poor Yorick Shakespeare Catalogue at bardcentral.com, for example, was until a few years ago accepting orders for a whole world of lovingly crafted Shakespeare 'Toys and Doohickeys'. Among them 'deliciously strong wintergreen mints in a Shakespearean tin (My Kingdom for a wintergreen mint!)', an 'Alas! Poor Yorick' Mug ('Our Yorick skull-in-hand logo on a hefty, 15oz ceramic mug with a large, easy-grip handle') and Shakespeare Stationery Cards ('Blank note cards with sticker quotes featuring more than two dozen quotations and celebratory greetings for all occasions').

Other useful knick-knacks included a Bawdy Mug ('this mug is downright dirty, if you're in the know') and a Bawdy Pillow ('A true inspiration for your boudoir or Cheapside sitting room. 100% cotton and machine washable').

Or how about the Hamlet Finger Puppet Set ('Now you can be playwright, actor and director, putting on countless productions') or the Little Shakespeare Toy Figure

('Each of these posable figures comes with a collectable, twelve-page, mini colour comic book chronicling William's crazy adventures!')? Other options include the Shakespeare Action Figure ('Articulated 5in tall hard plastic William Shakespeare action figure, with removable book and quill') and the Shakespeare Nodder ('To nod or not to nod, that is the question').

However, pride of place in the gallery of Shakespearean 'merch' surely has to go to the Shakespeare Little Thinker Doll. The advertising spiel for this remarkable creature runs: 'Are you tired of all those cute but essentially brainless "beanie" dolls? We were, so to offset the trend we designed the "Little Thinkers". Let the Little Thinkers add a little culture and humour to your life. 11in tall and oh, so smart!'

Unfortunately the catalogue stopped accepting orders in December 2007, forcing devastated Bard enthusiasts the world over to shop elsewhere for their memorabilia.

BIG BROTHER

Ignorance of Shakespeare seems to be a pre-requisite for any appearance on a reality TV show, and almost a formula for success. In Germany's first series of *Big Brother*, for example, one of the most popular participants in the show was called Zladko.

Zladko's ignorance was such that he became notorious for replying 'A shake beer?' when asked about Shakespeare. He didn't win the competition, but did make a hit single which went into the top ten. The song contained the line: 'I don't give a f*ck about Shakespeare or Goethe'.

Likewise, in the 2007 UK version of the reality TV show, data entry clerk Brian was teased by his housemates for his ignorance of Shakespeare. When asked by Big Brother whether *Babe: Pig in the City* was written by Shakespeare, Brian replied: 'I don't know who this geezer is who's meant to have written or directed all these things. Think it's *Babe: Pig in the City*, because they spoke normal in that. I don't know how William Shakespeare directed it though.'

Despite this, researchers at the show later revealed that Brian had taken a GCSE in English and so would therefore have had at least some acquaintance with Shakespeare. Whether Brian was therefore wilfully misleading his housemates about the depth of his ignorance of Shakespeare thus remains one of the great unsolved mysteries of the 2007 series.

5
THE LITERARY LEGACY

HOUSEHOLD WORDS

Libraries could be filled with the famous quotes and sayings that have come down to us through Shakespeare's plays and poems. All of the following words and phrases will be familiar to the modern reader, but would you have known in which play they originate?

Though this be madness, yet there is method in 't
(*Hamlet*, Act II, scene ii)

The lady doth protest too much
(*Hamlet*, Act III, scene ii)

Brevity is the soul of wit
(*Hamlet*, Act II, scene ii)

Can I desire too much of a good thing?
(*Hamlet*, Act IV, scene i)

True is it that we have seen better days
(*As You Like It*, Act II, scene vii)

But love is blind, and lovers cannot see
(*The Merchant of Venice*, Act II, scene vi)

Why, then the world's mine oyster
(*The Merry Wives of Windsor*, Act II, scene ii)

This is the short and the long of it
(*The Merry Wives of Windsor*, Act II, scene ii)

I cannot tell what the dickens his name is
(*The Merry Wives of Windsor*, Act III, scene ii)

The better part of valour is discretion
(*Henry IV, Part I*, Act V, scene iv)

He hath eaten me out of house and home
(*Henry IV, Part II*, Act II, scene i)

I'll not budge an inch
(*The Taming of the Shrew*, Act I, scene i)

But, for my own part, it was Greek to me
(*Julius Caesar*, Act I, scene ii)

Cry 'Havoc', and let slip the dogs of war
(*Julius Caesar*, Act III, scene i)

Et tu, Brute!
(*Julius Caesar*, Act III, scene i)

Ambition should be made of sterner stuff
(*Julius Caesar*, Act III, scene ii)

NOVELS AND SHORT STORIES

Brave New World
The ironic title of Aldous Huxley's dystopian novel comes from *The Tempest* (1607). Prospero's daughter Miranda, on seeing other people aside from herself and her father for the first time, exclaims:

> How many goodly people are there here!
> How beauteous mankind is! O! brave new world,
> That has such people in't.

Act V, scene i

Under the Greenwood Tree
Used by Thomas Hardy as the title of his 1872 novel, these lines come from a song in *As You Like It* (1599):

> Under the Greenwood tree
> Who loves to lie with me,
>
> And turn his merry note
> Unto the sweet bird's throat,
> Come hither, come hither, come hither:
> Here shall he see
> No enemy
> But winter and rough weather.

Act II, scene v

The Darling Buds of May
This title of H. E. Bates's novels and short stories about the Larkin family first appears in Sonnet 18:

> **Shall I compare thee to a summer's day?**
> **Thou art more lovely and more temperate:**
> **Rough winds do shake the darling buds of May,**
> **And summer's lease doth have all too short a date.**

The Winter of our Discontent
The title of John Steinbeck's last major novel, published in 1961 and panned by critics, these famous lines derive from *Richard III*:

> **Now is the winter of our discontent**
> **Made glorious summer by this sun of York.**

Act I, scene i

Something Wicked this Way Comes
The words of one of the witches in *Macbeth* form the title to Ray Bradbury's fantasy horror story of 1961. They are uttered just before Macbeth's arrival in the cavern – a scene that confirms the thane in his move to the Dark Side.

> **By the pricking of my thumbs**
> **Something wicked this way comes.**

Act IV, scene i

Mortal Coils

The title of a collection of short stories by Aldous Huxley (1922) derives from *Hamlet*. The words occur in Hamlet's first soliloquy, 'To be, or not to be', in which the prince ponders the possible afterlife:

> **For in that sleep of death what dreams may come**
> **When we have shuffled off this mortal coil.**

Act III, scene i

Time Out of Joint

Phillip K. Dick's novel of 1959 was the inspiration for the hit 1998 movie *The Truman Show*. The original lines are from Act I, scene v of *Hamlet*, after the prince has learned from the ghost of his father's murder. Here the film mirrors the play and Dick's 1959 novel – a superficially untroubled world conceals uncomfortable and only guessed-at truths that the protagonist has to uncover to regain his freedom. In Hamlet's words:

> **The time is out of joint. O cursed spite**
> **That ever I was born to set it right!**

Time Must Have a Stop

This Shakespearean quote, from *Henry IV, Part I*, is the title of another of Huxley's novels (1944). It appears in the haunting speech of the dying Hotspur, who has received a mortal wound from Prince Hal, restored to favour and fighting for his father against the rebels, on the battlefield of Shrewsbury:

> O, Harry, thou hast robb'd me of my youth!
> I better brook the loss of brittle life
> Than those proud titles thou hast won of me;
> They wound my thoughts worse than sword my flesh:
> But thought's the slave of life, and life time's fool;
> And time, that takes survey of all the world,
> Must have a stop.

Act 5, scene iv

The Glimpses of the Moon

Edith Wharton's novel, following on from her Pulitzer Prize-winning work *The Age of Innocence*, also takes a Shakespearean title. The original quote is from the scene in *Hamlet* where the prince confronts the ghost of his father and asks why he has returned to haunt him:

> **What may this mean**
> **That thou, dead corse, again in complete steel,**
> **Revisits thus the glimpses of the moon,**
> **Making night hideous…?**

Act I, scene iv

Tomorrow and Tomorrow and Tomorrow

The title of Kurt Vonnegut's short story comes from the dramatic closing scenes of *Macbeth*. Beset by enemies, the king breaks off from defying the approaching armies of Malcolm to respond to the news of his queen's death:

> **She should have died hereafter;**
> **There would have been a time for such a word.**
> **To-morrow, and to-morrow, and to-morrow,**
> **Creeps in this petty pace from day to day**
> **To the last syllable of recorded time,**
> **And all our yesterdays have lighted fools**
> **The way to dusty death.**

Act V scene v

Cod Latin?

The character of Pistol in *Henry IV, Part II* has some splendid muddled lines of faux Latin. In Act II, scene iv he gives his motto as *Si fortune me tormente sperato me contento*, which translates as 'If fortune torments me hope contents me'. By the fifth act of the same play the phrase has become *Si fortuna me tormenta, spero me contenta*.

SOUNDS FAMILIAR? MORE HOUSEHOLD PHRASES

There's daggers in men's smiles
(*Macbeth*, Act II, scene iii)

What's done is done
(*Macbeth*, Act III, scene ii)

All the perfumes of Arabia will not sweeten this little hand
(*Macbeth*, Act V, scene i)

How sharper than a serpent's tooth it is to have
a thankless child!
(*King Lear*, Act I, scene iv)

Nothing will come of nothing
(*King Lear*, Act I, scene i)

Have more than thou showest, speak less than thou
knowest, lend less than thou owest
(*King Lear*, Act I, scene iv)

'Tis neither here nor there
(*Othello*, Act IV, scene iii)

I will wear my heart upon my sleeve for daws to peck at
(*Othello*, Act I, scene i)

POETRY

As in film, novels and television, the world of poetry has witnessed its own fair share of Shakespearean borrowings.

Robert Browning

The nineteenth-century English poet Robert Browning was one of the leaders of this trend, taking lines from Shakespeare as a title for one of his most famous poems. 'Childe Roland to the Dark Tower Came' finds its genesis in medieval literature, but is also found in *King Lear*. Here it appears in a muddled-up song by Edgar, now disguised as Poor Tom:

> **Childe Rowland to the dark tower came,**
> **His word was still 'Fie, foh, and fum,**
> **I smell the blood of a British man'.**

Act 3, scene iv

Ogden Nash

Very Like a Whale, a collection of nonsense poems by Ogden Nash, comes appropriately enough from the third act of *Hamlet*, in a scene where Polonius is gulled into talking gibberish by Hamlet:

HAMLET
> **Do you see yonder cloud that's almost in shape of a camel? ... Methinks it is like a weasel.**

POLONIUS
> **It is backed like a weasel.**

HAMLET
Or like a whale.
POLONIUS
Very like a whale.

Act III, scene ii

Robert Frost

The title for 'Out, Out', a poem by Robert Frost, comes from *Macbeth*, Act V, scene i. Lady Macbeth, driven mad by her part in Duncan's murder, attempts to wash away imaginary spots of blood from her hands: 'Out, damned spot! Out, I say!'

Sylvia Plath

A strange song from *The Tempest* was the inspiration for the title of Sylvia Plath's 1958 poem 'Full Fathom Five'. The original words are those of the spirit Ariel, eerily echoing Ferdinand's grief for the father he believes has recently drowned:

> **Full fathom five thy father lies;**
> **Of his bones are coral made;**
> **Those are pearls that were his eyes:**
> **Nothing of him that does fade**
> **But doth suffer a sea-change**
> **Into something rich and strange.**

Act I, scene ii

Lines from Ariel's song also appear in Books I and II of T. S. Eliot's masterpiece *The Waste Land* (1922).

6
POWERS
OF DARKNESS

MAGICIANS – GLENDOWER AND PROSPERO

A belief in magic in Shakespeare's plays extends beyond the three witches in *Macbeth*. In Glendower in *Henry IV, Part I* and Prospero in *The Tempest*, the audience gets a glimpse of two magicians with a deep faith in their ability to fashion the world according to their desires – all through the power of magic.

Glendower bears witness to his own magical talents, claiming that his birth was marked by 'fiery shapes' in the heavens and earthquakes, and that he can 'call spirits from the vasty deep' and 'command the devil'. Unfortunately his knowledge of 'deep experiments' does nothing to impress fellow rebel Hotspur, who evidently holds such 'skimble-skamble stuff' in poor regard. He describes how the highly voluble Glendower delayed him for nine hours 'in reckoning up the several devils' names/That were his lackeys', and resentfully adds:

> ... Sometime he angers me
> With telling me of the moldwarp [i.e. mole] and the ant,
> Of the dreamer Merlin and his prophecies,
> And of a dragon and a finless fish,
> A clip-wing'd griffin and a moulten raven...

Act 3, scene i

For all Glendower's bombast, Prospero in The Tempest is a far more successful and convincing magician. It is left to Caliban to describe how Prospero's spirits appear to torment him 'sometimes like apes', 'then like hedgehogs' and then like adders to 'hiss [him] into madness'.

GHOSTLY PROTOCOLS

In the opening scene of *Hamlet*, Shakespeare provides his audience with a perfectly practical 'how to' guide for confronting ghosts. In the play Francesco, Barnado, Marcellus and Horatio are discussing an apparition that has been stalking the battlements of Elsinore Castle for the past couple of days when suddenly the ghost reappears. Shakespeare's stage directions and the reactions of the characters reveal much about seventeenth-century protocols for dealing with ghosts – protocols of which a modern-day audience may well be blissfully (and dangerously) unaware.

Always address ghosts in Latin

This is the reason Horatio – described as 'a scholar' by his companions – is urged to be the one to talk to the ghost. The tradition that ghosts and representatives of the spirit world are more likely to understand Latin persists to this day. Both exorcisms and the Black Mass, for example, are in Latin, and the association of Latin with magic and the spirit world has also endured: think of Harry Potter's *expelliarmus*, for example. In the event theatrical convention requires Horatio to speak to the ghost in English in the play (otherwise many in the audience would have failed to understand him) – but the point about Latin remains. In Hamlet's first meeting with the ghost in Act I, scene v, for example, he exclaims: 'Hic et ubique' (here and everywhere) – when urged by the disembodied voice of the ghost to swear to revenge his murder.

Ghosts do not speak unless spoken to

This is evident in the first scene of *Hamlet*, where Marcellus urges Horatio to 'speak to it' [the ghost] and again later in the scene where Horatio says:

> **Stay, illusion,**
> **If thou hast any sound or use of voice,**
> **Speak to me.**

In the event only the dead king's son has the power to make the ghost speak, and it is not until the fifth scene of Act I, in response to Hamlet's 'Speak. I'll go no further' that the ghost utters its first sound: 'Mark me.'

Cockcrow

On hearing a cock crow, ghosts will be forced to return to the underworld.

This is exactly what happens to the ghost in the first scene of *Hamlet*. In the words of Marcellus: 'It faded on the crowing of the cock.' This is also the basis for the belief, expressed by Marcellus in the same scene, that on Christmas Eve the cock crows all night so that 'no spirit dare stir abroad', thus preventing any evil from happening ahead of Christmas Day. As a result:

> **The nights are wholesome, then no planets strike;**
> **No fairy takes, nor witch hath power to charm.**
> **So hallowed and so gracious is that time.**
>
> *Act 1, scene i*

Presumably the reasoning here is that the cock's crow heralds the breaking of the dawn. Ghosts, only permitted to walk at night by the guardians of the spirit world, are fooled by the crowing of the cock into thinking that dawn is approaching, and so disappear.

Try to discover why the ghost has appeared

In Horatio's attempted interrogation of the ghost in the first scene of *Hamlet*, he runs through the most typical explanations for recurring ghostly apparitions:

1 The ghost needs something to be done for it, such as the burial of its body ('If there be any good thing to be done/that may to thee do ease and grace to me,/Speak to me')

2 The ghost is an omen ('If thou art privy to thy country's fate,/ Which happily foreknowing may avoid./O, speak!')

3 The ghost has buried treasure on its conscience ('If thou hast uphoarded in thy life/Extorted treasure in the womb of the earth,/For which, they say, you spirits oft walk in death,/Speak of it')

4 Unfortunately the cock crows and the ghost disappears before Horatio has a chance to reach a fourth possible explanation for its appearance – to demand revenge for its murder.

MORE GHOSTS AND GHOULS

Ghostly apparitions play a large part in Shakespeare. We have already
seen the methods Hamlet and Horatio have of dealing with the
appearance of Hamlet's murdered father, but there are other ghosts
that appear in the plays. Here are a few of them:

Banquo

In *Macbeth* the murderous king is confronted by the ghost of Banquo,
whom he has ordered to be assassinated along with his son Fleance.
In the event Fleance escapes, but the murderers succeed in cutting
Banquo's throat and leave him lying in a ditch 'with twenty trenched
gashes on his head'. Macbeth learns of this as he is hosting a banquet
(Act 3, scene iv), but his satisfaction at the plot's success is cut short
by the appearance of Banquo's blood-drenched ghost, who enters
the room and sits at the king's place at the table. Unlike Old Hamlet's
ghost Banquo is silent; only Macbeth is able to see him. The king's
first response on seeing the ghost paints its own grisly picture, though:
'Thou canst not say I did it; never shake/Thy gory locks at me.'

Julius Caesar

In *Hamlet* Horatio relates how ahead of the assassination of Julius Caesar, 'The graves stood tenantless and the sheeted dead/Did squeak and gibber in the Roman streets'. In Shakespeare's retelling of the emperor's murder, the ghosts also appear after the murder. In *Julius Caesar*, as in *Macbeth*, it is a guilty conscience that prompts the appearance of a wronged spirit: Brutus is confronted by the ghost of Caesar whom he helped to kill. As in *Hamlet*, Brutus must prompt the spirit to explain its presence:

> ...Art thou any thing?
> Art thou some god, some angel, or some devil,
> That mak'st my blood cold and my hair to stare?
> Speak to me what thou art.

Act 4, scene iii

Caesar then tells the tormented Brutus he will see him again on the battlefield, and disappears.

Richard III

When it comes to guilty consciences and ghostly apparitions, *Richard III* takes some beating. In Act V, scene iii of the play, on the eve of the Battle of Bosworth, the king is confronted by the ghosts of a full cast of 11 characters in whose deaths he has played a part. They are Edward, Prince of Wales, Henry VI, George, Duke of Clarence, Lord Rivers, Earl Grey, Sir Thomas Vaughan, Lord Hastings, the young Princes, the Duke of Buckingham and Lady Anne. Each of them curses the king, exhorting him to 'despair, and die!'

BLOOD AND GORE – *MACBETH*

Gore figures large in Macbeth – especially immediately after the murder of Duncan. In Act II, scene ii Macbeth enters 'carrying two blood-stained daggers'; he refers to his 'hangman's hands' before Lady Macbeth tells him to get water 'to wash [off] this filthy witness'. Later in the same scene Macbeth begins to fear the blood will never be cleaned; rather will the oceans turn red before it comes away:

> **Will all great Neptune's ocean wash this blood**
> **Clean from my hand? No, this my hand will rather**
> **The multitudinous seas incarnadine,**
> **Making the green one red.**

Lady Macbeth then smears the hands and faces of Duncan's sleeping grooms with the dead king's blood to implicate them as the murderers. Macbeth is later confronted by the bloody ghost of Banquo, whom he has had murdered, while his queen descends into madness – spending her final hours before committing suicide attempting to wash imaginary spots of blood from her hands.

BLOOD AND GORE – *JULIUS CAESAR*

The assassination of Julius Caesar in the play that bears his name is accompanied with enough gore to satisfy the most bloodthirsty of theatregoers. After Caesar has been brutally stabbed to death (he receives a more than adequate 33 stab wounds), Brutus urges his co-conspirators to cover themselves with the dead man's blood:

> **Let us bathe our hands in Caesar's blood**
> **Up to the elbows, and besmear our swords:**
> **Then walk we forth, even to the market place...**
> **waving our red weapons o'er our heads.**

Act II, scene i

DEMONS, FAMILIARS AND WITCHCRAFT

In *King Lear* Edgar, disguised as the madman Poor Tom, describes how 'the foul fiend' 'follows' and 'vexes' him – then makes reference to the six spirits or demons that haunt him. The names, some in a corrupted form, are taken from Samuel Harsnet's *Declaration of Egregious Popish Impostures*, a treatise on witchcraft and possession published in 1603. Poor Tom's demons include:

Flibbertigibbet
The 'foul fiend' responsible, according to Poor Tom, for 'the web and the pin' (i.e. cataracts) and harelips. The demon also 'squenies the eye' (causes squints), 'mildews the white wheat' (causes almost ripe wheat to rot on the stalk) and 'hurts the poor creature of the earth'.

Smulkin
Also described as a 'foul fiend' by Poor Tom. He is the madman's 'follower', so could be his familiar or facilitator in the spirit world. In Harsnet's *Declaration* Smulkin exits a possessed man's ear in the guise of a mouse.

Modo and Mahu
In Harsnet's *Declaration* the two are generals at the head of demonic armies. In contrast Poor Tom says they are alternative names for Satan: 'The Prince of Darkness is a gentleman; Modo he's called and Mahu.'

Fraterretto
Another name from Harsnet. Tom exclaims: '[He] calls me and tells me Nero is an angler in the lake of darkness.'

Hoppendance

A corruption of Harsnet's *Hoberdidance*. In *King Lear* Tom characterises the demon as a toad hidden in his stomach: 'Hoppendance cries in Tom's belly for two white herring. Croak not, black angel! I have no food for thee.'

Obidicut

Responsible for lust.

Hobbididence

The 'prince of dumbness'.

It is not just Poor Tom who has his familiars: the witches in *Macbeth* also have their demonic followers. In Act I, scene i the following exchange between the three takes place:

> **FIRST WITCH**
> **I come, Greymalkin.**
>
> **SECOND WITCH**
> **Paddock calls.**
>
> **THIRD WITCH**
> **Anon!**

Greymalkin and Paddock are usually glossed by editors as a grey cat and a toad respectively, while the 'anon' is sometimes interpreted as a response to the call of an owl – all three of which are traditional animal associates in witchcraft.

GROSS GOURMETS, PART II

A second famously grim list of ingredients goes into the pot in the notorious witches scene in *Macbeth*, Act IV, scene i. Here the witches use:

'poisoned entrails'

'toad that under cold stone/Days and nights has thirty-one' (i.e. a month-old toad)

'sweltered venom, sleeping got' (snake venom that's been sweated out in sleep)

'fillet of a fenny snake' (fillet of a snake that lives in either a fen or marshland)

'eye of newt'

'toe of frog'

'wool of bat' (bat hair)

'tongue of dog'

'adder's fork' (the forked tongue of an adder)

'blind worm's sting' (venom from a slow-worm – actually without venom in real life)

'scale of dragon'

'witch's mummy' (fragments of a mummified witch)

'maw and gulf/Of the ravined salt sea shark' (the stomach and gullet of a shark that's just finished eating its prey)

'root of hemlock digged i' the dark' (root of hemlock, a plant well known for its poisonous properties, dug up during the night when its poison was thought to be at its strongest)

'liver of blaspheming Jew' (see racism and anti-Semitism; anti-Semitism appears to have been a recurring feature of some of Shakespeare's plays)

'gall of goat' (gall, secreted by the liver)

'slips of yew/Slivered in the moon's eclipse' (slices of the yew tree, also poisonous, cut during an eclipse of the moon, a particularly inauspicious time)

'nose of Turk' (similar to the 'blaspheming Jew' in that a Turk would also not have been christened)

'Tartar's lips' (as above, but an inhabitant of the Russian and Mongolian steppes instead of a Turk)

'finger of birth strangled babe/Ditch-delivered by a drab' (finger of a baby strangled at birth (and so unchristened), delivered by a prostitute in a ditch)

'A tiger's chaudron' (tiger's entrails)

'baboon's blood' (the baboon was considered to be an especially lecherous creature)

'sow's blood that hath eaten/Her nine farrow' (nine being a particularly inauspicious number)

'grease that's sweaten/From the murderer's gibbet' (grease on a gibbet from the corpse of a convicted murderer)

BLOOD AND GORE – *CYMBELINE*

Cymbeline has its own unexpectedly gory moments. Imogen, awaking from a deep, drug-induced sleep, finds the headless corpse of what she believes to be her husband beside her. Unaware that it is in fact the decapitated body of her nemesis Cloten, she daubs herself with the corpse's blood.

BLOOD AND GORE – *TITUS ANDRONICUS*

Macbeth, Julius Caesar and Cymbeline all have their moments of bloodletting, as shown above – but the play with far and away the most gore has to be Titus Andronicus. Severed limbs galore combine with ripped-out tongues, rape, attempted infanticide and two lead characters cooked in a pie to make for probably the most gruesome viewing on the Elizabethan stage.

What's Eating Aaron?

Like Iago in *Othello*, Aaron in *Titus Andronicus* is the author of some of the nastiest and most vindictive plots in Shakespeare. He not only convinces the empress's sons to rape and maim Lavinia, but also tricks Titus into lopping off his own arm in the vain hope of saving his sons from execution. If anything, Aaron's motives are even harder to fathom than those of Iago. In Act V, scene i he tells Lucius how he duped Titus into cutting off his own arm and then: 'drew myself apart / And almost broke my heart with extreme laughter.' Later in the same scene he outlines what has to be the most tasteless practical joke imaginable, exclaiming:

> **Oft have I digg'd up dead men from their graves,**
> **And set them upright at their dear friends' doors,**
> **Even when their sorrows almost were forgot;**
> **And on their skins, as on the bark of trees,**
> **Have with my knife carved in Roman letters,**
> **'Let not your sorrow die, though I am dead.'**

Thoroughly unrepentant, Aaron's other 'notorious ills' include killing or devising how to kill, raping or plotting rape, accusing the innocent of crimes and setting friends at odds. He has also made 'poor men's cattle break their necks' and 'set fire on barns and haystacks in the night, / ... bidd[ing] the owners to quench them with their tears'. He is a thoroughly nasty piece of work.

BASTARDS

There are a lot of bastards in Shakespeare. Some are bastards in the traditional sense – illegitimate children born outside of marriage – but actually a good few of them are bastards in the modern sense of the word too.

Among the 'good' bastards are the Bastard of Orleans, one of the French leaders in *Henry VI, Part I*, and Philip (the Bastard) Faulconbridge from *King John*.

The 'bad' bastards include Don John, the dastardly brother of Don Pedro in *Much Ado About Nothing*, and Edmund in *King Lear*. Edmund is probably the biggest bastard of the lot: he not only dallies treacherously with the affections of two sisters, but also causes his own father to be tortured and blinded, orders the innocent Cordelia to be hanged and tries to kill his own brother.

In *Cymbeline*, meanwhile, Posthumus Leonatus comes to the unhappy conclusion that: 'We [men] are all bastards' after being fooled by the evil Iachimo into believing his wife Imogen has been unfaithful. He bitterly observes:

> **And that most venerable man which I**
> **Did call my father was I know not where**
> **When I was stamp'd. Some coiner with his tools**
> **Made me a counterfeit...**
>
> *Act 2, scene v*

One other type of bastard appears in Shakespeare. In *Henry IV, Part I*, Hal describes Falstaff's enjoyment of bastard, a type of sweetened wine from Spain.

7
COMING TO
A BAD END

INFANTICIDE

Macduff's young son is killed in the fourth act of *Macbeth*, but not before he utters a classic Shakespearean insult after hearing his father accused of treason: 'Thou liest, thou shag-haired villain!' The murderer's response is similarly ripe: 'What, you egg,/ Young fry of treachery!' Whether the punning on fry and egg was intentional is a different matter.

FAILED SUICIDES, PART I

In *King Lear* Edgar, disguised as the mad vagrant Poor Tom, describes the seven ways he has been tempted to suicide and thus damnation by the devil. He has been:

1 led through fire and flame

2 led through rivers ('through ford and whirlpool')

3 led over bogs and quagmires

4 the devil has 'laid knives under his pillow'

5 the devil has laid 'halters in his [Tom's] pew' (i.e. ropes with which to hang himself)

6 the devil has 'set ratsbane [poison] by his porridge'

7 he has been 'made proud of heart, to ride on a bay trotting horse over four-inched bridges to course his own shadow for a traitor' (i.e. the devil has tempted him to ride over dangerously narrow bridges in pursuit of his own shadow)

In Christian folklore ratsbane, knives and halters were the traditional gifts of the devil to those in despair. It was held to be in the devil's interest to tempt people to kill themselves, since it was believed that the soul of a suicide would go straight to hell.

The Most Alcoholic Death

The award for the most alcoholic death in Shakespeare goes to George, Duke of Clarence. In *Richard III* he ends his days by drowning in a large barrel of malmsey wine.

POISONINGS, PART I

Hamlet is the grandfather of all Shakespeare's poison plays. No less than four characters are done away in the final scene through the combination of a poison-tipped sword and a poisoned chalice.

Gertrude
The queen drinks from the poisoned chalice. Her last words are: 'The drink, the drink! I am poison'd.'

Claudius
The evil king who has murdered his own brother for the crown is stabbed with the poisoned rapier by Hamlet. He then receives a taste of his own medicine when forced by his nephew to drink poison

from the chalice. The king's last (ironic) words are: 'O, yet defend me, friends. I am but hurt.'

Laertes

Brother to drowned Ophelia and son to murdered Polonius, Laertes dies after being stabbed by Hamlet with his own poisoned rapier. He confesses his part in the poison plot and points the finger of blame at the king:

> '...lo, here I lie,
> Never to rise again. Thy mother's poisoned.
> I can no more. The King, the King's to blame.'

Act 5, scene ii

Hamlet

The prince, having been stabbed by Laertes, dies from the poison on the rapier. His final, haunting words: 'The rest is silence.'

POISONINGS, PART II

We have already seen that *Hamlet* contains no less than four on-stage poisonings. There is, however, still more – that of Old Hamlet, the king. This highly significant poisoning, despite taking place before any of the action begins, is actually the catalyst for everything that unfolds. In Act I, scene v the king's ghost describes how he has been slain by the 'juice of cursed hebenon' – hebenon being the folk name for henbane, juice of the plant *Hyoscyamus niger*. The ghost goes on to relate how he was poisoned and describes the grisly action of the henbane on his body – lines worth quoting in full if only for grim effect:

> **Swift as quicksilver it courses through**
> **The natural gates and alleyways of the body,**
> **And with a sudden vigour it doth posset**
> **And curd, like eager droppings into milk,**
> **The thin and wholesome blood. So did it mine.**
> **And a most instant tetter barked about,**
> **Most lazar-like, with vile and loathsome crust**
> **All my smooth body.**

The image is of blood being curdled by the poison (a posset was a drink made from milk curdled by wine or ale), while the king's skin becomes covered in a scabby crust ('barked about') like that of a leper. Leprosy was a disease greatly feared in the late sixteenth and early seventeenth centuries, as it had been since medieval times.

Shakespearean lore has it that this incident was inspired by the real-life murder of the Duke of Urbino in 1538, killed after his barber rubbed poisoned lotion into his ears. Henbane was also used in 1910 by Hawley Harvey Crippen (better known as the notorious Dr Crippen) to murder his wife.

GROSS GOURMETS, PART III

Shakespeare's *Titus Andronicus* wins the prize for leaving the worst taste in the mouth when it comes to gross gourmets, featuring as it does a truly horrific act of cannibalism.

In revenge for the killing of his two sons and for the rape and maiming of his daughter, Titus turns the empress's sons Chiron and Demetrius into the main ingredients for a pie to be served at a banquet in her honour. He uses his one remaining good hand to slit the two men's throats, while his daughter Lavinia holds "tween her stumps' the basin that collects their blood. Titus outlines his recipe for the pie as follows:

> **Receive the blood; and when that they are dead,**
> **Let me go grind their bones to powder small**
> **And with this hateful liquor temper it;**
> **And in that paste let their vile heads be bak'd.**
>
> *Act 5, scene ii*

In the bloody final scene of the play, the vengeful Titus enters
dressed as a cook. Upon being asked the whereabouts of Chiron and
Demetrius he declares:

> **Why, there they are both, baked in that pie;**
> **Whereof their mother daintily hath fed,**
> **Eating the flesh that she herself hath bred.**
> **'Tis true, 'tis true; witness my knife's sharp point.**
>
> *Act 5, scene iii*

His next act is to stab the horrified empress – presumably with the
same knife he used to kill her wicked sons.

FAILED SUICIDES, PART II

In the fourth act of *King Lear* the Earl of Gloucester tries to commit suicide by jumping off a cliff. In a moment of dark irony (Act 4, scene vi) he is prevented from doing so by Edgar his son – who earlier, disguised as Poor Tom, had described being tempted to suicide by the devil. In the event the blind Gloucester is tricked into believing he has jumped off a cliff and somehow survived, when in fact he has only fallen to his knees. As before, the theme of being tempted to suicide by the devil is made explicit. Gloucester is led to believe that 'some fiend' had taken him to the top of the cliff. Edgar describes the fiend as having eyes like 'two full moons', a thousand noses and 'horns welked and waved like the enridged sea'.

Ouch! Most Stabbed Character in Shakespeare

According to Octavius, Julius Caesar's body receives 33 stab wounds. Cassius, Casca, Brutus, Decius Brutus, Cinna, Metellus Cimber and Trebonius are among the culprits.

THE FATE OF KINGS

Kings and queens have a hard time in Shakespeare. Time and again in the history plays the playwright exercises his fascination with majesty, its burdens and rewards. On more than one occasion kings and queens come to a sticky end. Perhaps *Richard II* expresses it best just ahead of his meeting with Bolingbroke, his exiled usurper:

> For God's sake let us sit upon the ground,
> And tell sad stories of the death of kings:
> How some have been depos'd, some slain in war,
> Some haunted by the ghosts they have depos'd,
> Some poison'd by their wives, some sleeping kill'd.
> All murdered – for within the hollow crown
> That rounds the mortal temples of a king,
> Keeps Death his court…
>
> *Act 3, scene ii*

Some of the less fortunate kings include:

Richard III (killed on the battlefield)

Duncan (assassinated)

Lear (dies of old age and shock)

Macbeth (killed on the battlefield, then beheaded)

Hamlet's father (poisoned by his brother)

Richard II (killed by Exton, who mistakes Bolingbroke's off-the-cuff comments for a death warrant)

Henry VI (stabbed to death by Richard III)

STABBINGS, PART I

Anyone who thinks stabbings and street violence are something new does not know the sixteenth and seventeenth centuries, at least if Shakespeare's plays are any kind of guide. Plenty of characters in the plays get stabbed – often either by being assassinated or through mortal combat – and they pretty much all die. Here are just a few of the more memorable ones:

Duke of Clarence *(Richard III)*
Stabbed, then drowned in a vat of wine containing severed pigs' heads.

King Richard *(Richard II)*
Stabbed by Sir Pierce of Exton, who misinterprets the cry of new king Henry IV – 'Have I no friend will rid me of this living fear?' – as a command to murder the deposed King Richard.

Coriolanus *(Coriolanus)*
Aufidius, leader of the Volscians, incites a group of conspirators to kill the Roman leader. The final scene features Coriolanus's stabbing and death.

Henry VI *(Henry VI, Part III)*
Murdered in the Tower of London by the dastardly Duke of Gloucester, soon to become Richard III. Henry VI's indignities do not end there, however: Gloucester later seduces the king's daughter-in-law, Lady Anne, over his dead body (literally), having also killed her husband Edward, Prince of Wales.

Julius Caesar (*Julius Caesar*)

Caesar's stabbing is probably the harshest: his cry of 'Et tu, Brute' has entered the language as the stock response to an outrageous betrayal.

King Richard (*Richard III*)

Richard III gets his comeuppance for his murderous misdeeds on Bosworth Field, where he is killed by the Earl of Richmond, later Henry VII.

Hotspur (*Henry IV, Part I*)

The fiery Hotspur, son of the rebel Duke of Northumberland, meets his match in single combat on the battlefield at Shrewsbury with a redeemed Prince Hal.

Edmund (*King Lear*)

Edmund, arguably the nastiest piece of work in King Lear, meets his end in a duel with Edgar, the brother he slandered earlier in the play. Good triumphs over evil, making for an unlikely deathbed *volte face* from Edmund as he repents his many sins.

Emilia (*Othello*)

Reveals details of the plot against Othello and is stabbed in the back by her thoroughly evil husband Iago. Dies singing a poignant song about willows.

Lavinia (*Titus Andronicus*)
Definitely wins the award for the most put-upon character in
Shakespeare. Not only is her husband murdered in front of her, but
she is also raped and mutilated. Finally she is stabbed by her own
father in the climactic scene of the play.

Tamora (*Titus Andronicus*)
The Gothic queen is stabbed to death with a butcher's knife by the
long-suffering Titus in the final scene of the play. She dies knowing
that she has eaten her own sons after they were baked in a pie and
served up to her by Titus.

Titus Andronicus (*Titus Andronicus*)
Eventually even Titus gets his chips when the Emperor Saturninus
stabs him after learning of the meat pie plot. He is stabbed in turn
by Lucius, Titus's son.

SUICIDES

Suicide was a very big deal in the sixteenth and seventeenth centuries. Anyone taking their own life would be denied a Christian burial and a place in heaven – so to commit suicide was to be eternally damned. Contrary to popular belief, there are 16, more than the oft-quoted unlucky 13 suicides in Shakespeare's plays:

Romeo and Juliet
Both the lovers kill themselves, Romeo by poison and Juliet by stabbing herself.

Julius Caesar
Cassius convinces his servant Pindarus to assist him in committing suicide, while Brutus runs on to a sword held by his servant Strato. In the same play Brutus's wife Portia kills herself by swallowing hot coals. Titinius, a friend of Brutus and Cassius, also stabs himself.

Othello

The Moor stabs himself after learning, too late, of his wife Desdemona's innocence.

Hamlet

Ophelia's death is initially presented as an accident by the queen. However, as the play progresses it becomes increasingly clear that Ophelia has taken her own life after being driven mad by Hamlet's rejection of her and his murder of Polonius, her father. In Act V, scene i the priest says her death was 'doubtful', and that but for the king's order she would not have received a Christian burial.

Macbeth

Lady Macbeth's death in Act V is also considered a suicide. Malcolm describes how the 'fiend-like' queen 'by self and violent hands/Took off her life'.

King Lear

In *King Lear* Goneril, the king's daughter and wife of Albany, stabs herself after poisoning her sister Regan.

Timon of Athens

Timon's self-neglect can be taken as a form of suicide. Disillusioned by the hypocrisy of his false friends he withdraws from the world and at the end of the play is found dead in a cave – an apparent suicide.

Antony and Cleopatra

This has the biggest suicide count of Shakespeare's plays – a grim tally of five self-inflicted deaths. Eros, a follower of Antony, stabs himself rather than obey Antony's order to kill him. Antony is then left to kill himself. Charmian and Iras, Cleopatra's attendants, also kill themselves rather than contemplate a life without their mistress. But the award for most glamorous suicide probably goes to Cleopatra, whose asp-induced death goes down in Bardolatry as one of the most melodramatic and best.

King Lear

Cordelia's shocking death in Act 5, scene iii is an example of an attempt to disguise murder as suicide. Edmund's orders, that she should be hanged and her death made to look like suicide, are delivered explicitly in his commission:

> **To hang Cordelia in the prison, and**
> **To lay the blame on her own despair,**
> **That she fordid herself.**

What's Eating Othello?

Othello offers an unparalleled study into the destructive nature of jealousy. It also offers up some extremely quotable lines.

In Act III, scene iii of the play, for example, Iago, Othello's Machiavellian advisor, ironically warns against feelings of jealousy:

> **O! Beware, my lord, of jealousy;**
> **It is the green-eyed monster which doth mock**
> **The meat it feeds on.**

In the same scene after Iago has sown the seed of doubt about Desdemona's fidelity, Othello says:

> **I had rather be a toad,**
> **And live upon a corner of dungeon,**
> **Than keep a corner in the thing I love**
> **For others' uses.**

In Act III, scene iv Iago's wife Emilia observes:

> **Jealous souls will not be answered so;**
> **They are not ever jealous for the cause,**
> **But jealous for they are jealous.**

By the end of the play the green-eyed monster is triumphant.

HANGINGS

Bardolph is one of Falstaff's boon buddies in *Henry IV, Part I* and *Henry IV, Part II*. But in *Henry V* the king makes an example of Bardolph to deter the English soldiers from looting: he is hanged for stealing a woollen pax.

A hanging also lies in wait for the unfortunate Clown in *Titus Andronicus* when he delivers pigeons and letters to Saturninus. Death at the end of a rope is all the thanks he gets for his troubles.

As noted, the most tragic death by hanging is that of Cordelia in *King Lear*, murdered on the orders of the dastardly Edmund. Even the last minute confession of a dying and repentant Edmund is not enough to save Cordelia. She dies in the arms of her father, the reprieve coming an instant too late.

STABBINGS, PART II

More Shakespearean stabbings, including those from the sword-fests *Macbeth*, *Romeo and Juliet* and *Hamlet*, are:

Duncan (*Macbeth*)
Candidate for the goriest stabbing, Duncan's violent death in Act I resonates through the remainder of the play. The murder echoes in Macbeth's fear that 'all great Neptune's ocean' will not wash the blood from his hands, and in Lady Macbeth's frantic and deranged attempts to wash imaginary blood off her hands in Act V.

Banquo (*Macbeth*)
Banquo and his son Fleance are set upon by three murderers in the pay of erstwhile friend Macbeth. While Fleance flees, Banquo is struck down.

Lady Macduff (*Macbeth*)
More murders at Macbeth's behest, this time of another former friend's wife and family. Lady Macduff, last seen exiting stage left, dies after seeing her defiant young son stabbed to death by the king's murderous cronies.

Macbeth (*Macbeth*)
What goes around comes around in the final scene of the Scottish Play. Macbeth meets his nemesis Macduff and is slain after learning that his opponent was 'from his mother's womb/Untimely ripped'.

Mercutio (*Romeo and Juliet*)

Mercutio is the first casualty of a play preoccupied not just with young love, but also with sword-fighting and duelling. He is stabbed by Tybalt as Romeo attempts to separate them.

Tybalt (*Romeo and Juliet*)

Tybalt's death follows Mercutio's in short shrift as Romeo revenges the death of his silver-tongued companion.

Paris (*Romeo and Juliet*)

Romeo gains another feather in his duelling cap with the slaying of Paris before Juliet's tomb. All three eventually end up dead in the tomb, along with the body of Tybalt, Juliet's cousin.

Polonius (*Hamlet*)

The first death of many in this soliloquy-laden tragedy, and he only Shakespearean character to be stabbed while hiding behind a curtain.

Laertes (*Hamlet*)

Keen to revenge the deaths of his father and sister, Laertes takes on Hamlet in a duel. He is stabbed by his own poisoned rapier.

Claudius (*Hamlet*)

The fratricidal king gets a taste of his own medicine when stabbed with a poisoned rapier by Hamlet, his nephew.

Claudius (*Hamlet*)

The 'sweet prince' meets his maker at the point of the same poisoned rapier used to stab and kill Laertes.

BEHEADINGS

The Duke of Somerset appears among the Lancastrian faction in **Henry VI, Part II**, but towards the end of the play is imprisoned in the Tower of London. His head is carried onstage by Richard (later King Richard III) in the opening scene of Henry VI, Part III.

Macbeth ends in a bloody duel between the avenging Macduff and the Scottish king. Macbeth is killed and Macduff then appears holding the king's severed head aloft.

In **Cymbeline** Cloten's head is cut off by Guiderius, one of the British king's sons.

Monty Python Moments?

> Fourth citizen: Tear him to pieces; he's a conspirator!
> Cinna: I am Cinna the poet, I am Cinna the poet!
> Fourth citizen: Tear him for his bad verses, tear him for his bad verses!

The above, almost Pythonesque exchange takes place in *Julius Caesar* after Caesar's assassination. Here mob rule even extends to literary criticism, it seems.

The final scene of another of the Roman plays, *Coriolanus*, gives birth to another potentially inappropriate and unintentionally Pythonesque moment:

> All Conspirators: Kill, kill, kill, kill, kill him!
> [The Conspirators draw, and kill Coriolanus:]
> [Aufidus stands on his body]
>
> All Lords: Hold, hold, hold, hold!

FAMOUS LAST WORDS

'Et tu, Brute? Then fall, Caesar!'
Julius Caesar

'The rest is silence.'
Hamlet

'As sweet as balm, as soft as air, as gentle –
O Antony! Nay, I will take thee too:
What should I stay?'
Cleopatra

'Thus with a kiss I die.'
Romeo

'Commend me to my kind lord. O! farewell!'
Desdemona

'Killing myself to die upon a kiss...'
Othello

'A horse! A horse! My kingdom for a horse!'
Richard III

'And damn'd be him that first cries, "Hold, enough!"'
Macbeth

'The drink, the drink; I am poison'd!'
Queen Gertrude

'... Look on her. Look, her lips.
Look there, look there!'
King Lear

'**Demand me nothing; what you know, you know:**
From this time forth I will never speak a word.'
Iago, before being taken away for torture

In *Henry IV, Part I* Harry 'Hotspur' Percy does not even get to finish his
dying speech. It is left to the victorious Hal to provide the
concluding word: 'worms':

> '**But thoughts, the slaves of life, and life, time's fool;**
> **And time, that takes a survey of all the world,**
> **Must have a stop. O! I could prophesy,**
> **But that the earthy and cold hand of death**
> **Lies on my tongue. No, Percy, thou are dust,**
> **And food for ...**'

8
MUSICAL
ADAPTATIONS

MAKING MUSICALS

With their intriguing storylines, elaborate disguises and memorable characters, Shakespeare's comedies are a natural source for modern musicals. Songs, colourful costumes and repartee, often features of the original plays, translate well into the genre and have attracted some of the most famous composers and producers. A less obvious vehicle, the tragedies also have links to musicals, with some people believing themes from Disney's *The Lion King* to have been inspired by those of *Hamlet*. Even challenging plays such as *The Taming of the Shrew*, its attitudes at stark variance with modern sexual equality, has become a hugely popular musical, driven by humour and a compelling Cole Porter score.

Twelfth Night

Twelfth Night has been subject to a couple of rock opera re-renderings. Your Own Thing was a 'Summer of Love' retelling that premiered off-Broadway in 1968, featuring such timeless rock classics as 'No-one's Perfect, Dear', 'The Flowers', 'Somethin's Happenin' (Baby! Baby!)', 'Hunca Munca' and 'The Now Generation'. The musical revolves around 20-year-old twins Viola and Sebastian who, as in the Shakespearean original, are victims of mistaken identity. After they are separated in a shipwreck, Viola disguises herself as a man to audition for an all-male rock quartet 'The Apocalypse', whose lead singer Disease has been drafted to fight in the Vietnam War. Hilarity ensues as Sebastian is mistaken for Viola and vice versa before the confusion is resolved and the twins find their true loves.

The original production of Your Own Thing ran for a remarkable 937 performances at the Orpheum Theater, off Broadway. It also opened in London's West End and in Sydney, Australia.

A second musical remake came in the form of 2005's juke-box offering All Shook Up, which ran for 213 performances at the Palace Theatre on Broadway. The plot revolved around the same 'is-she-a-he-or-is-she-a-she' theme, but this time wove songs by Elvis Presley into the action. Unfortunately the show got a less than flattering first night review from the New York Times theatre critic Ben Brantley. Clearly jaded by rock musical adaptations, Brantley wrote: 'What you have just heard is the sound of a camel's back breaking.'

Hamlet

Hard to credit, but 1994's Disney offering *The Lion King* has been cited as a musical reworking of *Hamlet*. Here Simba's succession issues and his anxiety about his place within the 'Circle of Life' are said to mirror Hamlet's own Oedipal dilemmas. Unlike *Hamlet*, however, *The Lion King* had both a sequel and a part prequel/partmidquel (*The Lion King 1½* and *The Lion King II: Simba's Pride*), as well as an award-winning score featuring Elton John.

The Comedy of Errors

The Boys from Syracuse, taking *The Comedy of Errors* as its inspiration, won plaudits as the first musical adaptation of a Shakespeare play. Featuring lyrics by Lorenz Hart and music by Richard Rodgers, it debuted on Broadway at the Alvin Theater on 23 November 1938 and ran for 235 performances. Song titles include 'I Had Twins', 'Dear Old Syracuse', 'Let Antipholus In' and 'Oh, Diogenes!'

Sheep's Guts

Twelfth Night's 'If music be the food of love' is one famous quote about music and romance in Shakespeare. However, in Act II, scene iii of *Much Ado About Nothing*, Benedick has a far more cynical take on the ability of music to fire the imagination: 'Is it not strange that sheep's guts should hale souls out of men's bodies?' Here sheep's guts are the material with which Renaissance instruments would have been strung.

Love's Labour's Lost

Kenneth Branagh's 2000 version of *Love's Labour's Lost* may have deserved some credit for being the first musical adaptation of Shakespeare's most difficult and inaccessible play – but it was still roundly panned by critics. Among the reviewers' less favourable comments were 'unfathomably awful' (David Edelstein), 'smug' (Kenneth Turan) and 'inadequate in every way' (Stanley Kauffmann).

Less critical, however, was *Variety* reviewer Derek Elley, who wrote of the film: 'Anyone with an open mind and a hankering for the simple pleasures of Tinseltown's Golden Age will be rewarded with 90-odd minutes of often silly, frequently charming and always honest entertainment.' Despite his generous comments the film was still a flop.

The Taming of the Shrew

Cole Porter's musical *Kiss Me, Kate* is by far the most successful musical adaptation of a Shakespeare play, sweeping the 1948 Tony Awards with Best Musical, Best Author of a Musical, Best Composer and Lyricist, Best Costume Design and Best Producer of a Musical. It ran for a record 1077 performances after opening on Broadway at the New Century Theater on 30 December 1948.

9
WILL THE REAL WILL SHAKESPEARE PLEASE STAND UP?

THE MAN BEHIND THE PLAYS

So who really wrote the plays? Was it the philosopher Francis
Bacon? Perhaps it was Shakespeare's contemporary, Christopher
Marlowe? Or maybe even Sir Walter Raleigh or Elizabeth I?
One of the great things about Shakespeare is the relative scarcity
of detail about his private life – leading to popular films such
as *Shakespeare in Love* (1998), which presents a fictional love
story involving the young playwright as the inspiration behind
Romeo and Juliet. The absence of real information leaves us with
a void that just begs to be filled with conspiracy theories about
who he really was.

One such theory states there is no way that Shakespeare could possibly have written the plays. He was the son of a rural glove-maker and had never been to university – nor as far as we know even travelled further than London. How could such a man possibly have written with so much insight, erudition and authority across such a broad spectrum of topics and genres? Only a thorough grounding in the classics, for example, would have prepared the way for a playwright to tackle *Julius Caesar*, *Antony and Cleopatra*, *Coriolanus* and *Titus Andronicus*. Shakespeare, according to contemporary playwright Ben Jonson, had 'but little Latin and less Greek'.

Likewise, in an age where most of the rural population barely ventured more than a few miles from their place of birth, how could a native of sleepy Stratford know enough to base 22 of his plays in locations far beyond the British Isles? The same argument runs true for the intimate knowledge of courtly rituals on display in Shakespeare's plays – and what about the playwright's evident familiarity with contemporary theories on witchcraft and the occult (see *Macbeth* and *King Lear*, especially)? Then there are the frequent references to theology and the Bible to contend with, as well as an awareness of foreign languages (for example, Latin in *Love's Labour's Lost* and French, in particular in *Henry V*), an understanding of astrology and even an apparent intimacy with the complex workings of the legal world.

Given these apparent deficiencies in background, it is no surprise that modern academics have dredged up a surfeit of candidates for the 'real Shakespeare'...

THE REAL WILL SHAKESPEARE?

Edward de Vere

One of the candidates for the 'real' Shakespeare, according to
scholarly naysayers, is Edward de Vere, the 17th Earl of Oxford. He
was not only well travelled, wealthy and educated, but also had a
fledgling literary career that was mysteriously cut short just as
Shakespeare's got under way. Here the critical verdict ranges from
'plausible' to 'no way', with apparently little common ground in
between. The verdict? This has potential, but the theory has been
widely ridiculed by the academic establishment.

The recent film *Anonymous* (2011), starring Rhys Ifans as Edward de
Vere and Vanessa Redgrave as Elizabeth I, presents a fictional account
of the earl's life. In it Oxford is the author of all Shakespeare's plays,
as well as the lover of the queen and father of one of her illegitimate
children, later the Earl of Southampton. A young actor, William
Shakespeare, takes the credit for de Vere's plays, which the nobleman
cannot acknowledge; he proves an unattractive character,
blackmailing de Vere to pay for the building of the Globe theatre and
possibly involved with the murder of Christopher Marlowe, who has
discovered the plays' true authorship. Full of historical inaccuracies
and implausible scenarios (de Vere apparently writes *A Midsummer
Night's Dream* at the age of eight or nine), the film was largely derided
by critics, with kinder reviews conceding that it was 'ridiculous but
not dull'.

Francis Bacon

A second candidate for the 'real' Shakespeare is Francis Bacon, the ultimate Renaissance heavyweight whose interests ranged from philosophy to alchemy, theology to politics. Vastly erudite, well travelled and well connected, Bacon would certainly have had the background and the knowledge to have taken a stab at writing the odd play or two. Conspiracists have also found cryptograms in Shakespeare that could point towards Bacon as the author. One such is an anagram in the made-up word 'honorificabilitudinatibus' in *Love's Labour's Lost*, which can be rearranged to read: *hi ludi F. Baconis nati tuiti orbi* (translated as 'these plays F. Bacon's offspring preserved for the world').

Given this apparent weight of evidence, the generally accepted verdict on the Bacon-as-Shakespeare theory is that it is plausible but unlikely. Apart from anything else, Bacon was phenomenally productive in his own right without having the time to pen 30 or so plays of his own.

Kit Marlowe

A third candidate for the 'real' Shakespeare is Christopher 'Kit' Marlowe, the 007 of the Elizabethan theatrical world. Not only was Marlowe a wonderfully talented playwright, but he also allegedly did a bit of spying on the side – a consideration that adds sufficient spice to the story to make conspiracy theorists drool. The argument runs that Marlowe's mysterious death in a pub brawl in 1593 was a cover-up, and that the playwright – because of the necessity of maintaining the fiction of his death – was obliged to write under the Shakespeare pseudonym from then on. Here the verdict on Marlowe-as-Shakespeare is that it's plausible – other than the inconvenience of having to account for the plays already written by Shakespeare prior to Marlowe's death in 1593.

Other possibilities

Other notable candidates for the 'real' Shakespeare include (in decreasing order of probability) William Stanley, Earl of Derby; Ben Jonson; Thomas Middleton; Sir Walter Raleigh; Queen Elizabeth I.

So who was the real Shakespeare? Perhaps Ralph Waldo Emerson came closest in *Shakespeare; or the Poet* in 1904 when he wrote: 'Shakespeare is the only biographer of Shakespeare; and even he can tell us nothing.'

Shakespeare's Bed

An inordinate amount of space and time has been devoted to scholarly discussions on the question of Shakespeare's bed. The reason for this is the entry in Shakespeare's will that reads: 'Item, I give unto my wife my second best bed with the furniture'. Clearly this begs the question: why did he leave his wife only his second best bed and who got the best one? The generally accepted answer is that the best bed was reserved for guests to the house, whereas the second best bed is where Shakespeare and his wife would usually have slept.

SHAKESPEARE AND HIS ACTING 'FELLOWES'

We know that William Shakespeare was attached to a theatre troupe known as 'the Lord Chamberlain's Men' – and later, following the accession of James I, as 'the King's Men'. As an 'in house writer', he was contracted to write probably two new plays a year for his company, bearing in mind the talents and limitations of the actors around him. Richard Burbage – son of the founder of 'Burbage's company' (an early incarnation) who arranged for the building of the first Globe Theatre in Southwark – was a celebrated tragic actor who took on the great roles of Hamlet, Macbeth, King Lear and Othello, as well as the Machiavellian Richard III. Burbage was obviously capable of portraying such roles with psychological subtlety – a new style of acting then replacing the more traditional 'declaiming' favoured by another great Elizabethan actor, Edward Alleyn.

Female roles were were inevitably more problematic, depending as they did on the talents of of teenage boys. Young romantic heroines such as Juliet or Silvia were were relatively straightforward for these actors. More mature, complex female characters – such as Lady Macbeth, Cleopatra, Volumnia, the mother of Coriolanus, even the evil Goneril and Regan – would have required an exceptional range and were presumably written for specific boys. Another important member of an Elizabethan acting troupe was the clown; he often provided a bridge with the audience, dancing a 'jig' at the end of outdoor performances and extrapolating beyond his script. Will Kempe was the first clown in Burbage's company and roles such as Dogberry, full of chat and vigour, reflect his skills. His successor Robert Armin was a different character – more serious, contemplative, even sombre, as shown by the more complex Fools in *As You Like It, King Lear* and *Twelfth Night*.

Shakespeare seems to have had close relationships with his acting colleagues, and in his will he made final bequests of rings to three of them: Richard Burbage, Henry Condell and John Heminge, said to have been the first Falstaff. Burbage died in 1619, only three years after Shakespeare, while Condell and Heminge edited the first-ever collected edition of Shakespeare's plays, published in 1623. Anyone who has enjoyed watching or reading Shakespeare's plays today is deeply in their debt.

SHAKESPEARE'S PLAYS

Shakespeare wrote 37 plays between *c.*1590 and 1612. They are commonly divided into tragedies, comedies, histories, the so-called 'problem plays' and the late romances, written towards the end of Shakespeare's career and revealing preoccupations with reconciliation and loss. They draw upon and reinterpret a range of sources, from the *Chronicles* of Holinshed to the classical writings of Plutarch, and boldly address England's turbulent recent history as well as offering powerful insights into what it means to be human. Today the plays capture the imagination of audiences all over the world and have been translated into hundreds of languages, as well as into media such as film and television totally unknown to Shakespeare. It is a remarkable legacy.

Have you seen them all?

TRAGEDIES

Titus Andronicus
First performed 1593

Romeo and Juliet
1594

Julius Caesar
1599

Hamlet
1600

Othello
1604

King Lear
1605

Macbeth
1605

Antony and Cleopatra
1606

Timon of Athens
1607

Coriolanus
1607

COMEDIES

The Comedy of Errors
1592

The Taming of the Shrew
1593

The Two Gentlemen of Verona
1594

Much Ado About Nothing
1594

Love's Labour's Lost
1594

A Midsummer Night's Dream
1595

As You Like It
1599

Twelfth Night
1599

The Merry Wives of Windsor
1600

HISTORIES

Henry VI Part II
1590

Henry VI Part III
1590

Henry VI Part I
1591

Richard III
1592

Richard II
1595

King John
1596

Henry IV Part I
1597

Henry IV Part II
1597

Henry V
1598

Henry VIII*
1612

PROBLEM PLAYS

Troilus and Cressida
1601

All's Well that Ends Well
1602

Measure for Measure
1604

* Probably written in collaboration with John Fletcher

LATE ROMANCES

Pericles
1608

Cymbeline
1609

The Winter's Tale
1610

The Tempest
1611

The Two Noble Kinsmen*
1612

* Probably written in collaboration with John Fletcher

ACKNOWLEDGEMENTS

To Soph for putting up with me and for Monty for when he's old enough to read. Thanks to Ben B for suggestions and to Luke for beer and sympathy.

Euphemisms from Eric Partridge's excellent *Shakespeare's Bawdy*.

Epitaph

Shakespeare's epitaph appears over his tombstone in the chancel of Stratford's Trinity Church:

> Good friend, for Jesus's sake forbeare
> To digg the dust enclosed here.
> Blest be ye man that spares thes stones
> And curst be he that moues my bones.